MY BRATVA CHRISTMAS

XXXMAS

MIKA LANE

HEADLANDS PUBLISHING

The last thing I expect when I take a job in a new town is to end up living with three smoking hot roommates.

Who also happen to be personal trainers.

They are so out of my league, and I am so out of my element.

But I can't afford to live alone in San Francisco, so have resigned myself to sharing.

Apparently, these guys like to share too…

Overhearing them say I'm cute gives me a nice ego boost.

But I want to get in shape, and they'll only help me under one condition…

I have to do *whatever* they tell me to, *whenever* they tell me to do it.

Instead of scaring me, the thought of being at their beck and call sounds hot.

And once they start with their naughty demands, I want them to never stop.

They work me hard in the gym and everywhere else.

This whole roommate situation just put a new spin on 'sharing.'

COPYRIGHT

Copyright© 2022 by Mika Lane
Headlands Publishing
4200 Park Blvd. #244
Oakland, CA 94602

Cover by Cormar Covers

thereof may not be reproduced or used in any manner whatsoever without the express written permission of the publisher except for the use of quotations in a book review.

<u>Like deals and other cool stuff?</u>
<u>Sign up for my newsletter!</u>

CHAPTER ONE

GRISHA

"LOSER HAS no idea what's coming."

I'm not so sure tonight's mark, or 'loser' as Artem puts it, is that clueless. Personally, I don't like to take things for granted. That's how a person ends up dead. And in our business, shit like that happens all the time.

I throw Artem a side-eye. The man's confidence never wavers. Not even when, staring at the ass of a woman sauntering past us, he ends up on the receiving end of a scowl that would have a lesser man's balls crawling up inside his abdomen in retreat.

She looks away just as quickly, and I figure he

probably fucked her ages ago and never called afterward.

She really shouldn't be all that surprised. Everyone knows Artem's modus operandi. It's the same all us guys operate under.

When the woman and her perfect bottom are out of view, he turns to me. "Grish, you always have to interrupt me when I'm appreciating the female form. Why must you do that?" he huffs, taking a swig of his scotch.

I'm also choking down, or trying to, the shitty scotch that Sergey, our host and said 'loser,' has the fucking balls to serve us. He can afford better. Much better. Cheap bastard. I'm tempted to say something to him, that his cheap-ass liquor is an insult to not only me but also all his guests, but it would be pointless. Before the evening is over, it won't matter. He won't be buying any more scotch, ever, whether the cheap or good shit.

Still irked, which is pretty much baseline for Artem, he turns to Valentin, my brother, and gestures at the art donning the walls of the gallery where we're attending an upscale Christmas Eve party. "Do people actually pay money for this shit?" he asks, sullen and disbelieving.

He has a point. For fuck's sake, the six- and

seven-figure paintings on offer look like something a six-year-old could do.

In the dead center of the room, people are drooling over the artist responsible for said art, lining up to talk to him like he's proffering blessings or some shit from a high altar, like the goddamn Pope or Dalai Lama.

Yeah, I have to agree with Artem on this point. I have nothing against art. It's just that this stuff is not my jam. "No kidding. Think about it. If you buy one of these… paintings," I say, unsure what else to call them, "you gotta look at them every fucking day."

My brother shrugs. "I like them. I do." He looks around approvingly, like the other fake-ass poseurs in the room.

The fucker always has to contradict me. If he wasn't my younger brother, I would have beaten him senseless long ago.

"Yes," he says thoughtfully, as if he might pull out his checkbook right there on the spot. "I can see one or two of these hanging in the house. I don't mind abstract impressionism in the right setting."

What the fucking fuck.

"And how do you know so much about art, Val?" Artem asks, laughing.

Valentin gives him dirty look. "I took an art history class in college for an easy A. Talk about a way to meet hot babes. I got so much pussy out of that course I could hardly walk."

I roll my eyes. "That's not because of all the pussy, but from the gonorrhea."

"Fuck off you jealous prick," Valentin says, laughing.

He's the only one of the three of us to get a university degree. He'd insisted on it before agreeing to join the family business, and since he was always my father's favorite, he got the old man's blessing. But I don't begrudge him much. He is, after all, my only brother.

A strong blast of perfume assails my nose, adding to my already-shit mood. I hate overly fragranced women. Actually, I hate overly fragranced anything.

This night's just getting longer and longer. And it's goddamn Christmas Eve.

"Gentlemen," a scratchy voice purrs as a large, undeniably fake breast presses against my elbow, "I don't think I've seen you here before. Friends of Sergey's?" a woman asks, sizing us up and trying especially hard to get a look at my wrist watch. In these circles, one's watch is a critical calling card.

It never ends, the sizing up. The assessments. I

consider saving her time and getting right to the point.

Yeah, bitch, we're loaded.

But that doesn't mean we're going to let you suck our dicks. At least not tonight. We're here to take care of some business. Messing around with gold diggers will have to wait for another time.

"He's one of our… business partners," Artem says, clinking his scotch against her champagne flute full of pink bubbles.

I shoot him a look warning him not to encourage her, but he conveniently ignores me. Artem's number one goal in life is finding receptacles for his dick. He's so obsessed with getting laid he'd probably fuck his sister if he had one.

As the woman learns about our association with Sergey, her unnaturally blue eyes—tinted contacts are popular among her type—reveal her unabashed approval, as if we need it. Or could give a fuck. The dollar signs passing through her mind, like scrolling numbers on a slot machine, are as easy to spot as her fake tits. Yes, Sergey's loaded. So if we work with him, we must be too.

A correct assumption.

But Sergey's rich because we made him rich. Not because he sells ugly fucking art.

"My name is Paisley," she says, extending her hand. "Happy holidays."

Artem takes it before she realizes we really don't give a shit about meeting her. He's just laying the groundwork for future pussy.

"I'm Art," he says. "This is Grisha, and his brother Val. Happy holidays to you, Paisley."

Fake-ass name if I ever heard one. She probably sprang from the American Heartland with a given name like Jane or Mary.

She turns to me, the last one of us she should be bothering with. "Grisha. Now that's an interesting name. What's its origin?"

Fine. Acceptable question. People ask it all the time.

"It's Russian. Our parents were from Russia." I gesture between Valentin and myself.

Artem can explain his own goddamn family tree.

This news makes her nipples hard. They poke through her white silk halter top, announcing her interest like a flashing neon sign.

"Oooh, Russian," she coos, "just like Sergey. I *love* Russian men," she says, stroking Artem's bicep since he's the only one paying her any attention.

For Christ's sake, lady, why don't you just lift

your skirt and bend the fuck over so we can get on with it?

Women on the make at events like this bug the shit out of me. They're out for something, be it money, status, or whatever the fuck else they want that week. Which doesn't mean I don't fuck them. I do, because I'm a bastard that way. But tonight, that shit is off the table.

And Paisley needs to hit the road if she knows what's good for her.

Turns out she does exactly that just a few seconds later.

A redhead I've been watching all evening—just because there's no *fucking* tonight doesn't mean I can't enjoy the scenery—comes rushing out of Sergey's back office where the catering shit is set up, holding a nice-looking bowl of shrimp cocktail to replenish an empty one. I glance over at the lonely buffet table she's hurrying toward, which Sergey undoubtedly paid a fortune for—again, with our money—and check out the high-end eats. The only thing anyone's touching is the shrimp.

People rarely eat at these things. It's ironic but the richer people are, the less they eat. And tonight, the buffet table's deserted in spite of some fancy shit I can't even identify.

The redhead is clearly working the Christmas

Eve event in some capacity, rushing around like a maniac making sure everything's perfect. That makes it easy to watch her, oblivious as she is to the guys and me, and really, all the party guests. But this time, when she emerges from the back, I catch her eye and smile.

And, she's so caught off guard that she trips, flying in my direction. With a bowl of shrimp cocktail.

I try to catch her, which I mostly do, and she fortunately remains upright. But the cocktail sauce, on its way to the floor, spills onto my hand and over my wrist, soaking the cuff of my bespoke dress shirt as well as my watch.

My fucking expensive watch.

"Goddammit," I say. My expletive causes the redhead to jump back, terror crossing her face before turning into abject embarrassment.

"Oh my god, oh my god, oh my god," she cries, crouching to scoop the mess off the floor, then attempting to wipe off my wrist with a nasty-looking rag.

I step back so she can't make more of a mess and take her by the arm to pull her back to her feet.

"Oh god," she cries again. "Look what I've

done," she says, her face bright pink, her bottom lip trembling.

I want to be pissed. That's my normal MO. In fact, I'm nearly always pissed. I'm just a grumpy guy that way. It serves me well in the work I do, although Valentin regularly reminds me that my shitty outlook will probably put me in an early grave. He's forever reading about staying healthy, reminding me to eat right and keep my blood pressure low.

I ignore him, of course.

But this time, the rage that naturally lives so close to the surface of my being doesn't make itself known.

Which is strange.

Maybe it's the holiday spirit.

Regardless, I feel something like compassion for this girl, clearly just trying to do her job. And now that she's made a mistake, well, she looks like she's about to jump off a bridge or something.

I can kind of relate. I'm hard on myself too. Have been for as long as I can remember. That's the way it goes when you're the oldest of immigrant parents.

My folks saw some awful shit in Russia—they mostly only talked about it in code, I guess to spare my brother and me—and they wanted to make sure life in America didn't repeat the past.

That manifested as a mother and father expecting nothing less than perfection from me, their oldest son. It was a foregone conclusion that I'd follow Papa into the 'family business' as he called it. He and his cronies from the old country established themselves in a few industries when they arrived in America, where a lack of oversight and ability to move large sums of cash undetected made it easy to basically carry out the same shit they had been in Russia. But America was better, Papa always said. Fewer crooks.

Or, *not as many crooks*, as Valentin says.

Sure, America has its share of criminals, but the percentage, compared to the population, is nowhere like it is in Russia, thanks to the turmoil caused by the fall of the Soviet Union.

Plus, here, there's no price on my father's head, like there was at home.

So, coming to America was a good move for the whole family, as long as we sons fell in line, which we eventually did.

"What's your name, sweetie?" I ask the redhead when she's back on her feet, staring at the red sauce covering my hand.

Fuck if she isn't tall—nearly eye-to-eye with

me thanks to the high heels she's teetering in. Her lithe figure is tucked into a slim black dress that fits her like a glove, and she is wearing tasteful diamond stud earrings. Maybe I'll make an exception to my no-fucking rule for the night. A little Christmas present to myself.

After business is addressed, of course.

Hearing me say 'sweetie,' Artem rolls his eyes long and hard, but because he's behind the girl, she has no idea he's mocking me. Although she'll find out real quick if I give Artem the shoulder chuck he deserves.

Her gaze meets mine and she stumbles when she sees how intently I'm looking at her. I can't help it. She's dressed so simply, almost like a school librarian, but her bright red hair and plush lips make her, by contrast, deliciously kissable. And more.

The paradox of which has captured my attention. Big time.

"Um, I'm Lily. And I'm so sorry, sir. My company will gladly pay to have your clothes cleaned, and if you'd like to come back to the sink with me, I'll clean that cocktail sauce off your watch," she babbles, clearly freaking about the possibility of having ruined my watch because she knows there's no way in hell she or her company can afford to replace it.

I'm charmed. Which is unusual for me because I'm a cynical fucking bastard. "Lily, I am sure the watch will be fine. Look, it's just a little spatter," I say, unhooking it from my wrist and showing it to her.

She has no idea how much it's worth because *I* have no idea what it's worth. But it's probably safe to say it's more than she earns in a year.

"I'm happy to clean that for you, sir," she says. She looks at me so earnestly with those big blue eyes that my cock twitches.

Get yourself under control, asshole.

But something about a pretty girl looking to me for approval, not to mention calling me *sir*—well, her guilelessness shoots straight through to my dick, leaving me picturing her balancing on top of me, slowly lowering herself onto my—

"I'll be right back, sir. I'll clean this right off. It's the least I can do."

She snatches the watch right out of my hand while I'm busy having dirty thoughts about her, and disappears with it.

I probably wouldn't have let her make off with it if I'd had a second to stop her, but thinking with my little head gets me into trouble every time.

"Goddammit," I say, watching her disappear out of view. "You know how much that fucking thing is worth?" I grumble to no one in particular.

Valentin slaps me on the back. "Chill out, brother. I'm pretty sure she's good for it. Besides, you can always get another."

"Thanks, Val. Thanks for fucking nothing."

"Merry Christmas to you too," he laughs.

"Hey," Artem interrupts, "if you two can stop bickering for a moment, we have shit to take care of."

He finishes his drink and sets the crystal glass on a nearby table. He adjusts his trousers like he's tucking his shirt in, but I know better. He's checking his weapon.

That's Artem. He might be cocky, but he knows when to be cautious. And prepared.

He waves across the room, and when I turn to look, I find he's greeting Sergey, who weakly smiles back at us with a wave of his fingers. Yeah, we are about the last people on Earth he wants to see tonight. Can't blame him. He knows there's a price to pay for dipping into the cash he's been laundering for us. He just doesn't know what that price will be, nor when it will be time to pay it.

But he's about to find out. The man's number is up. Christmas Eve be damned.

"I say we wait until the party clears out. I don't like excess collateral damage," Artem says.

I shake my head. "Fuck the collateral damage. Sergey's been warned once and didn't make things right. Personally, I don't think people should even get one warning. Sends the wrong message. Makes us look weak," I say.

Like I have to share my opinion. The guys know where I stand.

We both look at Valentin as if he's the tie-breaker and has more sway than I do. Which he does not. "I'm with Grisha. Sergey's a bum."

That's the brother I know and love. His vote may not count for a lot but I appreciate the buy-in.

"Well, shit," I say, rubbing the empty spot where my watch should be. "Look who's heading our way right now. And are those fuckers behind him his backup?"

My hand flies to my gun and rests there. Ready and waiting.

Sergey is weaving through all the idiots salivating over the bullshit art hanging on his walls, pausing to shake hands and slap people on the back, like he's some fucking rockstar.

"Guys," I say, "let me get my watch first. Wait here."

I take a step in the direction of where Lily the

redhead ran off to, but before I get any further, Artem shouts my name. When I turn to look at him, he has his gun drawn. Reflexively, my hand grabs mine, even though I'm still assessing the situation.

It doesn't take long to understand why Artem yelled for me.

Sergey's only a few feet away, a big a smile on his fake-tanned face.

With a gun in his hand.

CHAPTER TWO

LILY

I WASN'T sure whether the man was going to hit me, kiss me, or bend me over to have his way with me.

That's how oddly he reacted when I dropped shrimp cocktail on him.

Seriously. When he first saw the stuff all over his wrist, and then his watch, he looked for a moment like his head would explode. But in a matter of seconds, after he'd looked me over, his expression transformed. Like he understood how terrible I felt and was even a little sorry for me.

It was an accident, of course. He knew that. I knew that. The guys he was hanging out with knew that. But you never know how rich people at these parties are going to behave. Some are nice and others are total dicks.

But that comes with the territory when you work for an event planning company, particularly one of the best in New York City.

I don't like pity, but if that's the price of avoiding the rage of some good-looking rich guy at a ritzy gallery party, I'll take it.

Now, I just have to figure out how to clean his darn watch. I consider running it under the water, but I don't want to risk damaging it. I'm pretty sure these expensive watches are pretty much waterproof, but I can't take the risk. I wipe at it with a clean towel, but that just pushes the red stuff into its nooks and crannies.

Good move, Einstein.

If only I had a toothbrush. Yes, that's what I need.

So. Freaking. Embarrassing. But when it comes down to it, tonight's klutziness isn't much of a surprise. I am exhausted nearly to the point of tears, having worked for the last ten nights straight, putting on all manner of holiday parties for affluent New Yorkers. I've been out until two a.m. most of those nights, yet my boss still expects me in the office by nine. Sure, the holiday season is a busy time of year like it is for any reputable party planner, but the pace this year is going to put me in an early grave.

Why don't I just say no, like any normal person would? But *no* isn't a very practiced part of my vocabulary. I want my boss to like me. See me as a big contributor, an invaluable part of the team. And with most of the other girls from the office gone for Christmas, visiting family and skiing with boyfriends, this is my opportunity to shine. I want a promotion. More responsibility. And of course, money.

Going away for the holidays isn't my thing, anyway. I don't actually have anywhere to go, when it comes down to it. I seldom speak to my father and in order to spend time with my sisters, Charleigh and Evie, I'd have to see him. So, I'm sending them all the Christmas gifts I can afford—Charleigh's in school and is perpetually broke, and Evie is a high schooler trying desperately to fit in. Besides, they've been through some hard times they've come out the other side of, so I like to spoil them. It's not like my father does much to help them.

Hell, I'd move them here to live with me if I could afford it. But life in the big city is expensive, and I don't earn enough to feed three mouths. In fact, I barely earn enough to feed myself. Ramen noodles are a staple of my diet, except for the times when I can take home leftover catering from the parties I work. Which, fortunately, happens a lot. Otherwise, I might starve or at least come down with scurvy.

So, with nowhere to go for Christmas, it just makes sense to work, and given the time of year, the work is pretty much endless. The holidays fly by for me this way, leaving me little time to worry about being a workaholic or think about all I'm missing out on, like having a social life or meeting guys.

I glance around the gallery storage room, the staging area for this evening's fancy party, searching for some small tool to get the damn watch clean so I can get back to work.

And have another excuse to talk to the handsome man whose wrist it had come off. I can't lie. He's beyond gorgeous, and the way he looked at me had my knees shaking. I always like to imagine the rich men I meet at these things might ask me out, and in fact, one once did. But before we went on our date, I consulted my dear friend Google, and found out the creep was married.

I kept the date with him but stood him up, and boy, was he mad. It was the most fun I'd had in a long time—messing with a cheater. Sad thing is, he'll probably just do it again to someone else.

I've never dropped anything on a guest before. Wouldn't it figure, the first time I do, it's on a perfectly-chiseled master of the universe type, hanging out with equally gorgeous friends. It's like good looks beget more good looks. Seriously, his dark eyes and dimples, and the thick black hair brushed away from his face, it all shows off the incredible bone structure nature blessed him with. And it's not lost on me that he's wearing one of those high-end suits I often see men at our parties in. Further, when he removed his watch, I spotted a pair of the gold Cartier cufflinks my boss just gave her husband for their anniversary.

Yeah, she can afford such things.

Because of the people we throw parties for, I've developed an eye for the items rich people like, as if these objects are secret name tags for an underground club. The kind where my type is never invited, only allowed to watch through the window, from the outside.

Wanna know how rich I am? Look closer because I'm not going to make it easy for you, is what these symbols of affluence seem to say.

So, I finally get the idea to snag a toothpick from the caterer's stash and pick out the last of the now-dry, sticky cocktail sauce from the watch's bezel. I've never even heard of a Patek Philippe, the brand name adorning the watch face, but I'm certain it's something I'll never own.

I'm going to add this to my mental inventory of 'rich people things.'

I wipe the watch down one last time as quickly as I can, because I want to see its owner again. Maybe he'll even let me place it on his actual wrist.

How pathetic am I?

I'll admit I've been spending that evening, in between replenishing the buffet table and spilling shrimp cocktail, spying on the man and his friends. I have a lot of downtime at these events. I'm basically there to make sure everyone else does their job. But sometimes I pitch in. Thus, the spilled shrimp.

I know full well I am so not in the league of guys like these, but hey, looking is free. I do think from time to time how nice it would be to have my own Steady Eddie. Someone to hang out with every now and then, grab dinner with, watch Netflix with, and who also thinks I'm kind of pretty and occasionally tells me so. Is that too much to ask?

As evidenced by my sad record of occasional online dating, apparently, I *am* asking too much.

Most of the guys I meet online are looking to get laid—not that there's anything wrong with that. I enjoy a romp in the hay just like any other girl. But if guys *aren't* looking to get off, they are the opposite extreme, attaching themselves to me like leeches, ready to walk down the aisle after two dates.

Isn't there anyone in between? Like, normal?

Like *me*?

So, I've sworn off online dating for the holidays, knowing my availability is severely limited because of work, anyway. And because I have pretty much no life outside work, my boss takes full advantage of me. I'm the one always available for last-minute bookings, the one willing to work on holiday weekends, and the one who never complains, no matter how much crap is loaded onto my shoulders. But that's okay. I'm satisfied, if not mostly content with my life. Truly. It's predictable, and that's comforting. I'm not much for surprises, or winging it, or spur of the moment.

It's nearly midnight. The gallery party should be wrapping up soon, which means I can head out, leaving the caterer with clean-up duty. I plan to pack myself a big doggie bag of leftover food from the buffet, and once home, pull on my PJs, put my feet up, and unwind with a movie like *Love*

Actually, my holiday season go-to. Given that tomorrow is Christmas, I actually have a day off. In fact, I don't have another gig until New Year's Eve, unless the boss has some sort of last-minute party scheduled. I'll be back in the office the day after Christmas, of course, but there will be a nice break from the late nights.

Although, I don't mind the nights all that much. It's interesting to see how a certain faction of New Yorkers live, people I would otherwise never rub elbows with. Not that I really *do* rub elbows with them. We're just in close proximity. But because I'm there to work and not socialize, I'm essentially invisible. I like it that way. I have no ego about the whole thing. I'm just grateful to be floating about a party without the expectation of making clever small talk, worrying if some bitchy lady is assessing the cost of my dress, or having to ward off the wandering hands of male guests.

It's like being a ghost.

I spot a tray of desserts that the caterer forgot to put out. So, I drop the watch into my pocket and grab them. Even if the party is winding down, maybe last-minute grazers will eat some of this stuff the gallery paid so much for.

But just before I push the door open, the floor shakes and a rat-a-tat explosion sears my eardrums. I instinctively bring a hand up to one ear, and jostle the tray in my other.

What in the hell was that?

This particular party hadn't hired out for a fireworks display. Which is alarming. We usually handle such details, in part because we're always sure to hire the best in town. If my boss finds out the gallery owner went around her, he'll end up on her black list. She has so much business she turns away clients who don't play by her rules. Personally, I wouldn't mind never coming back here. The gallery owner is a weird dude with a fake tan and overly white teeth.

Another *boom* competes with the DJ's house music as if they're in a contest to see which can be louder. It's a toss-up, amazing considering the fireworks are outdoors, as fireworks always are.

I exit the storage room and the first thing that strikes me is the smell of smoke. Wait, not exactly smoke. But something like it.

What's going on?

Did some bonehead actually set off fireworks indoors? What a major no-no. Cripes, the gallery owner could lose his business over something like this. Another event planning company in the city once provided its guests with sparklers at a party. The sparklers set off not only the fire alarm but also the sprinklers, ruining the floor and walls of an old historic building. Needless to say, this company is no longer in business.

Armed with my desserts and about to chew someone out about fire codes, I step into the gallery only to trip. Again. For the second time that night, a tray of food goes flying out of my hands. This time, I am falling right behind it, and there's no handsome man to catch me. As I go down, the white, twinkly lights around the tall, skinny Christmas tree blur thanks to the speed of my descent.

Just no. Please. Not again.

More concerned about the desserts than myself, I watch a dozen perfectly-formed peach pavlovas bounce off the tray in the direction of the floor. Why is the universe messing with me? And what message is it trying to send?

And as I follow the pavlovas, wishing I could wipe out with half the finesse they are, I land on something soft and squishy, putting my hands out just in time to prevent a face-plant.

What. The. Fuck.

I have tripped over, and am now sprawled on, a *body*.

Like a *human* body.

Why is someone on the floor of the gallery? Am I not the only klutz tripping over things?

A run pops in my pantyhose, zipping up the back of my leg like a little tickle, all the way to my thigh, and I scramble to get up to try and figure out what in god's name is going on.

That's when I look around the gallery and see that the body I tripped over is not the only one on the floor. In fact, for as far as I can see, the place is littered with bodies in varying positions. Unmoving. Not making a sound.

As if they might be sleeping, passed out, playing some sort of weird rich people game… or dead.

And the red stuff on the floor. Oozing red stuff that looks a lot like… blood. There are literal puddles of it, expanding, inching along like thick creeping vines, crawling slowly but steadily as if trying to reach some sort of equilibrium. And the smell. Strangely metallic, aside from the thinning smoke odor. Both fill my nostrils. The air doesn't stink, not exactly, and yet I don't understand why I suddenly want to vomit.

It's odd, the things that blow through the mind when confused, like a list with two columns. It could be *this*. But it's not *that*. Denial, acceptance, then denial again, reconciling something unfathomable when it's right there, in plain sight.

I squeeze my eyes shut, just for a moment, hoping that when I open them again, I'll find I'm hallucinating or having some sort of silly nightmare, having dozed off out of pure, overworked, holiday exhaustion.

But when I open my eyes, the bodies are still there, and for as far as I can see. A scream is stuck in my throat just like my feet are stuck in place. Actually, my thoughts are stuck, too, unable to make sense of what's going on, and what I'm supposed to do about it.

That's when a clicking sound from my right snaps me back to reality.

The good-looking guy from earlier, the one I dumped shrimp on, whose watch is in my pocket, is still standing, as are his two friends, just next to him.

Pointing guns. The three of them.

At me.

CHAPTER THREE

VALENTIN

I SLAM my brother's arm with the barrel of my gun.

"We're not doing this, Grish," I snarl, in part because I know what he's thinking and it pisses me the hell off, and also because I want to snap him out of a reflex that has gotten him in trouble on more than one occasion.

My quick action is successful, because his gun no longer pointed at the redhead. Instead, he turns toward me with frenzy in his eyes, letting me know I've not gotten completely through to him yet. I'm all too familiar with that look. I grew up with it.

"I'll kill you, so help me—" he shouts, raising his hand to take me down.

But Artem jumps in, and just in time. It's not that I can't defend myself against my brother, it's just that I don't unless I absolutely have to. Most days, reason is better than force, and thanks to Artem, Grisha is on his way to being under control again. At least I think he is. Sometimes it's better to be confronted by a non-family member.

Our attention returns to the redhead, the one Grisha flirted with earlier, and who, until a moment ago, he was ready to shoot dead like the rest of the poor bastards lying all over the gallery floor.

She, however, has not recovered from our threat. While his gun is now lowered, her eyes remain wide with horror, and while her lips are moving, there is no sound coming out of them. I've seen that sort of reaction before. She's had the living shit scared out of her. It will take her a few minutes to recover. This sort of thing is to be expected when you happen upon a room littered with dead bodies. Not to mention, have guns pointed at you.

To put it plainly, she's freaked the fuck out.

In spite of Artem's intervention, my brother raises his gun again in reflex. This time, instead of knocking his arm down, I speak evenly. Calmly. Quietly.

"Grish, we are taking her with us," I say.

It's no coincidence I initiated the shooting when she was out of the room, and my intention is now dawning on him.

He looks at me like he's considering my words. It's a good sign. I've successfully distracted him from his impulsivity.

And in a perfectly normal reaction to the shit-show around her, the redhead gasps, finally jolted out of her initial shock. "No, no, no," she begs, suddenly able to speak. "I… I'll stay here. I can't go with… you."

Artem takes her by the upper arm, and she tries to twist out of his grip, but her feet slip in the blood covering the gallery floor and she has no leverage. Not that she could escape him, anyway.

For a moment, I feel for her, not unusual for me. I'm the one in the group with the least rage. I'd rather we carried out our work with a minimum of conflict. I don't enjoy taking out people who aren't complying with our… business practices. It gives me no joy, unlike some of the other men who do the work we do.

And this woman—what was her name?—looks like a nice girl trying to make sure the gallery party comes off without a hitch. She had no freaking idea what she was walking into when she arrived to work this evening.

Unlike most other people here.

Who either ran when the shooting started or took a split second too long in drawing their own guns, and now lie on the gallery floor in a thickening carpet of red ooze.

Grisha directs her toward the exit. "Lily," — *that's* her name— "my brother is right. You need to come with us. It's not safe for you here."

We don't explain any further. She doesn't need to know that the target of our attack, Sergey, somehow managed to escape. Of course, the fucker sacrificed all his henchmen, hiding behind them like the nasty little coward he is.

I fucking hate a man who can't own up to his shit.

The scream of the inevitable police sirens gets louder, so I grab Lily's other arm and between Artem and me, my brother bringing up the rear, we steer her out of the gallery and to our waiting SUV, complete with dark, tinted, bullet-proof windows.

Once inside, sandwiched between the two of us, Lily covers her face with her hands, as if by wishing hard enough, her nightmare might end.

And behind her hands, she's incoherently mumbling.

Turning around from the front passenger seat, Artem sighs in frustration. He doesn't like complications, and an unexpected guest is always a complication. And a risk. "Lily? Please quiet down," he says.

She removes her hands from her face and draws her lips into a thin line, her emotions morphing from terror to a modicum of indignant anger. This is when they get combative, not that I'm really worried. She doesn't stand a chance against one of us, never mind all three.

"What am I doing here? You can't just… kidnap me, after *murdering* all those people," she says, unsuccessfully trying to hide her trembling voice.

I want to tell her it's normal to be scared. That we're just doing our job.

But I don't. I know from experience it won't help.

I steal a sidelong glance at her, and even through the drama, her red hair is still neatly slicked back into a low ponytail. There is a spot of blood on her face, where she must have touched herself after falling, and her hands are pretty much covered in the drying, cracking shit. Fortunately, she either hasn't noticed, because when she does she'll freak, or she *has* noticed and is more concerned about other things.

She's actually quite pretty, this Lily, so different from the other women at the party with their flashy clothes and jewels. It's like she took a page out of a handbook on elegant minimalism or something, with her black, fitted sheath dress, matching high heels, and sleek hairstyle.

I know that look. It's what women wear when they don't have a lot of money, but want to look chic, nonetheless. I don't meet a lot of women like this, but when I do, they catch my attention.

As piggish as it sounds, I've always wanted to fuck a girl like this, one who I can see writhing under me like I'm giving her something she's never had. One who acts shy at first, but then opens like a beautiful flower as I initiate her into a new level of sexuality, one she never knew was possible.

She'd be nothing like the women I normally bed, for whom sex is ridiculously performative. A means to an end.

That end being snagging a guy with money, and if she's really lucky, who's not half-bad looking. Yeah, I was over chicks like that. They bored the shit out of me.

Grisha looks past Lily toward Artem and me. "What do you want to do about that fucker,

Sergey? I'm thinking he won't be hard to find. You know how stupid he is."

Lily's eyes widen as she looks from one of us to the other. We pay her no mind. At the moment, we have higher priorities.

"I'm so tired of that fucker's shit," I say. "He's been digging himself a grave for a long time now, and this latest stunt has really shortened his life expectancy. I'm willing to bet he's decamped to New Jersey, already building a little army to take us out before we can get him."

I turn to Lily. "This is why we need to keep you safe, at least for now. Sergey will be coming after us, and that includes you."

From the streetlights shining into the car, I can see her eyes filling with tears. "But… but I didn't do anything. You know I didn't. I… I just want to go home. Can't I please go home?" she asks, the hands resting in her lap clenching and opening, then clenching again.

Damn, she's a nice-looking woman. It occurs to me I might regret taking her along on our adventure. Could lead to trouble. Perhaps it would have been easier to just let Grisha take her out like everyone else at the party. Artem was usually the one who thinks with his dick, not me, and I have no doubt he's surprised I invited along an unplanned-for guest.

Which means I'll need to keep an eye on her. She's pretty much my problem. The guys don't even have to tell me that.

Which I'm okay with.

It's something I look forward to.

CHAPTER FOUR

LILY

How?

It keeps repeating in my mind like a broken record.

How did I get into this predicament?

How did I happen to be in the wrong place at the wrong time?

How did these guys decide I should be saved rather than sacrificed?

And how will it all end?

Sergey, the gallery owner, did something to these guys. That much is easy to figure out. And these guys resolve issues by killing people. Lots of people. I figured that out too.

Pretty simple conclusions to draw.

But who are they? Who is Sergey? Does my boss know the kind of people these men are? Did she throw me to the wolves? Does she think so little of me, that everything about me is expendable?

I mean, I never expected us to be best friends, the boss and me. I am well aware that her Christmas present to me this year was a re-gifted scarf, one she probably forgot a client sent to her the previous Christmas. I didn't forget, though. I was the one who opened the mail that day.

And all those people in the gallery. Dead, and on Christmas Eve of all nights. Do they have family at home waiting for them? Gifts under their trees? Plans to have friends over for a holiday dinner?

While the guys talk about Sergey, I wonder what the cops will do when they arrive, most likely only a few minutes after we left, by the sound of the sirens. Maybe they'll be shocked like I was. Maybe not. Cops probably see stuff like that all the time.

Me, not so much. Except on TV.

And now here I am, sitting between two broth- ers. The Criminal Brothers, I'll call them. Not to their faces, of course. No need to poke a bear. But that's what they are, including their friend sitting up front.

Even if they are perfect specimens of male beauty. Even if every time one of them looks at me, my heart makes a little leap, and I don't mean from the shock of seeing dead people all over the floor.

How can I find criminals attractive? That's sick. Purely sick. Sure, I was admiring them all night, but that doesn't mean I want to go home with them. Willingly or unwillingly. And here I am, getting a free ride to god knows where, like they're doing me some kind of favor.

Saving my life, *my ass.*

Shame washes over me at the same time Valentin's thigh presses against mine. In a typically clueless manspread, he leans on my leg until my knees press together, the tingling feeling at the apex of my thighs intensifying to where I have to swallow a gasp when we hit the bumps on the lousy New York City streets.

Sure, Christmas decorations like garlands and banners hang from the streetlamps, but they don't erase the potholes and uneven pavement. And these signs of the holiday season, usually making me cheery and hopeful for a better new year, are suddenly naïve. Provincial. Silly. Did the person or people who hung them realize someone who'd witnessed mass murder was going to be looking at their handiwork and wishing it wasn't there?

It's like they're laughing in my face, that my holiday just went from merely crummy and uneventful to completely and totally fucked up.

Hiding my wanting reaction doesn't succeed though, and Grisha glances at me, I am sure assuming I'm upset at being kidnapped. Which, of course, I am. Let them think that. Let them think I am scared to death, because I actually am.

But please don't let them think our proximity has my hormones raging, not to mention my imagination.

Why didn't I just stay in the storage room? Why did I have to mistake gunfire for fireworks? How stupid is that?

If I had an ounce of brains, I'd have realized *oh my god, guns!* and run to hide. It would have been so easy. Just tuck myself behind some of the crap stuffed in Sergey's storage room and wait until the cops arrive.

How did everything in my life bring me to this moment, this insane, unexpected moment? I am a nice girl. I got away from my toxic father and put myself through college. I found an apartment in New York. I worked hard in a job I hoped would eventually reward me, if not monetarily then at least with promotions, not to mention free food. Maybe I'd even gain enough experience to open my own party planning company someday.

Guess all that's off the table now. How the hell will I come out of this alive? What if I'd just gone somewhere for Christmas instead of trying to please my boss? What if Sergey had hired a different company for his gallery party?

What if an asteroid had hit the earth this morning?

Get a grip, idiot. So many what ifs, and none of them make a damn bit of difference. The fact is, I'm in trouble, my life is in danger, and I have no freaking idea what to do about it.

Except to maybe reason with these men?

Their conversation about Sergey the gallerist ceased for a moment. I grab my opportunity.

"Um, do you think we could talk about this?" I ask, using my best dealing-with-difficult-clients voice. "If you could please just let me go, I'll head home and forget I ever saw you. If the police question me, I'll say I saw nothing—because I really did see nothing—and that everyone was dead when I came out of the back room. I don't want any trouble, just like you don't. Maybe pull over right here on this corner. I can get home from here."

They look surprised that I continue to make my case. But what the hell else can I do?

What if I never see my sisters again? They need me. I can't let that happen. I'm the support that's gotten them to where they are today, and that cannot come to a screeching halt. My dad will do nothing to help them.

Please god. Just let me get through this, and I will save Charleigh and Evie.

I try to swallow but I'm dry. So very dry. "Wh… what do you say? Can you at least think about it?" I ask in a trembling voice.

Surely, they'll listen. Consider my plea.

"Hey. Hey, I have an idea," I continue to babble. "I can leave town. That's what I'll do. Go back to where I grew up. My dad has a pawn shop. I can work there. You'll never see or hear from me again. I'll even tell you where it is. You can check up on me."

Silence.

But I'm not deterred, and continue. "What do you think? You'll let me go, right? Please. You don't understand. I have two younger sisters who need me."

A soft chuckle comes from one of the guys. Which one, I'm not sure. But Valentin, sitting on my right, pats my leg. "Can't do that, Lily. But good try. You could be a lawyer, you know. You are very convincing. And persistent."

Not enough, apparently.

"Look, you seem like a nice girl," he continues, as if his words might actually provide comfort.

Gee, thanks.

"You're not part of that world, those people left behind at the gallery. They're not nice people," he says. "You were in the wrong place at the wrong time. But that's okay. You'll be fine, because we're protecting you."

How is *kidnapping* me *protecting* me?

"He's right," Grisha says. "You're not like those other… people. We couldn't leave you behind. They would have come after you, Lily. You don't deserve that."

I don't see how I deserve *this*, either. And who'd come after me? They're all dead. Except Sergey, apparently.

But he hired my company. He knows my boss.

"There's another reason you're with us, Lily… we want to get to know you better," Valentin adds.

What the hell. Are these guys unaware that today's women expect to have a say in who we get *to know better*? In what world do people make this decision for me?

I didn't think these guys were anyone I was

destined to hang out with, per se, but they seemed nice enough at the party, and were certainly good-looking. Who the hell knew they were… whatever they hell they are?

What *are* they, exactly?

But there's no point continuing to argue. The time on the car's dashboard says after one a.m. At this point, and I've been awake since almost six a.m. the previous day. My head is heavy, and my thoughts are fuzzy. I don't want to think any more.

Maybe if I just doze off, I'll wake and find I'm just having a nightmare.

But one thought nags me, and it's that since tomorrow, or actually today, is Christmas Day, no one will be looking for me. Not my boss, because I have the day off, not any of my coworkers, because they're out of town, and not my sisters, because they've already opened their gifts from me and will be spending the day with our father.

No one in the whole world will know there's anything wrong except these three guys who have taken it upon themselves to 'save' me, which is total BS. The only saving I need is to be dropped off at my front door so I can enjoy Christmas Day alone, like I'd planned, like I do every year.

"Can I ask you a question, Lily?" Artem asks from the front seat.

My eyelids are getting heavy, but even in my extreme drowsiness I try to stay alert. So, I nod. "Yes. Sure," I say politely.

"What are you doing working Christmas Eve, Lily? Don't you have any people to be with? Isn't there anyone you ought to be home with?"

And that's what it boils down to. I don't even answer the man. It's obvious that if I *did* have a place to be, I'd freaking be there.

So now my kidnappers know what a loner I am, what a loser I am, and that *no*, I don't *have any people.*

I have my work. That's about it.

But at least I make an honest living, unlike these... whatever they are.

My thoughts spin until they become a mish-mash, like someone changing the radio station so fast, all you hear is that unpleasant jumble of shrieky sound, and thoughts slam-dance around my head with no intention of helping me through my messed-up predicament.

The SUV leaves the city for a freeway, I think heading north, and in spite of myself, my eyes fall closed and my head, so very heavy, falls to my right and lands on Valentin's shoulder.

The collision of my face against his suit jacket startles me awake, and my head snaps back to its upright position. But he turns to me and catches my eye, the first time I've really looked directly at him since we've been in such close proximity.

God, he's perfect. It makes it hard to hate him.

"Lily, here," he says, gently pulling me toward him. "Rest your head on me. Get comfortable. It's okay."

He actually places his hand on the side of my face, guiding me onto his shoulder and, in spite of myself, it feels nice to rest, and he smells really good besides. I need to chill so badly, to close my eyes for a little while and forget the worry swirling around me.

The white noise of the car on the open road, even though we are speeding away from the city, is soothing, rocking me to sleep, and now that I have a perch for my head, it's impossible to keep my eyes open. I can no longer stay alert, ready for any opportunity to save myself, and I slowly accept that I am absolutely screwed, probably beyond the point of no return.

CHAPTER FIVE

ARTEM

WHAT THE FUCK is Valentin thinking?

As soon as we're at the safe house, in another hour or so, and the redhead is tucked away, I plan to give him a piece of my mind.

Our situation is already precarious enough. The very asshole we set out to eliminate last night fucking got away, in spite of the fact that we left a gallery full of people dead and bleeding all over the floor. Sure, we hit the road before the police arrived—we always manage to do that—but it was a close goddamn call, and for all our effort, Sergey is still alive, living off the money he stole from us, and leaving us looking like a bunch of pussies to the other factions in the region.

This will not do. Not at all.

I can understand Valentin's wanting to take the girl with us. She's beautiful. Stunning, even. And yet understated. The way she slunk around in that tight black number she had on. Even though it was high-necked, long-sleeved, and came down below her knees like a fucking nun's outfit or something, it left little to the imagination. The outline of her perky tits and the slight bounce of her behind as she tottered around in her sky-high heels is the stuff of many a man's dreams. She was covered and yet revealed everything.

So close, and yet so far.

That shit drives me crazy.

Other chicks I usually come across let a little too much hang out. No, scratch that, they let *every-thing* hang out. Tits, ass, even pussy if they can get away with it, crossing and uncrossing their goddamn legs like Sharon Stone in *Basic Instinct*. There's nothing left to the imagination with these women, and I mean nothing. Nothing exciting to discover as you peel off their clothes in preparation for a fuck. They all have the same Botox treatments, the same breast implants, and the same waxed pussies. These even smell the same, as if their parents sent them to the same charm school that instructed them about the proper perfume to wear to land a rich man.

It bores the fuck out of me. Not to say I don't go home with them on the frequent occasion my balls need emptying. But after the deed's done, I only stick around long enough to not be a total asshole.

Of course, I can play nice when I want to. Why burn bridges? I might want to fuck the same girl twice, someday. It hasn't happened yet, but it could. Although, in New York, the supply of fresh pussy is nearly endless. So, I don't lose sleep over shit like that.

But this redhead, the one sacked out in the back of the SUV, with her head sweetly resting on Valentin's shoulder, well, she's different. Honestly, we never should have brought her with us when we hit the road—I'm sure we'll end up regretting it—but I can understand Val's curiosity about her.

She's beautiful and sweet, especially with the way she spilled that cocktail sauce on Grisha, and yet she was working Christmas Eve. Why wouldn't a pretty girl like her be off with an adoring boyfriend, who's showering gifts on her in a tasteful Upper East Side apartment, the kind with a round-the-clock doorman and separate service elevator?

It boggles the mind.

After a two-hour drive, the last couple miles to reach the safe house are over rutted dirt and gravel roads, designed to ward off all but the most nosy—or stupid—people, and the bouncing of the SUV drags Lily out of her deep sleep. But as soon as the car stops and the security lights scream into view, she closes her eyes and is asleep once again. Valentin eases her out of the vehicle, and I carry her into the house to one of our guest rooms. I put her down on the bed and just as we pull off her high heels, she pushes herself up on her elbows, ready to start swinging.

"Don't... don't touch me," she shrieks, kicking at Grisha with her torn pantyhose-covered feet.

I like a feisty woman. The kind who puts up a fight, even if it's an act. And Lily's thrashing, in that long tight dress of hers, is waking up the old cock and balls, even though I'm so tired I could fall asleep standing up.

"Calm down, for Christ's sake! Where's my watch?" Grisha yells after she lands him a swift kick to the chin.

His head snapped back like a jack-in-the-box's.

She scrambles up to the head of the bed,

drawing herself into a protective ball. "Leave me alone," she wails.

What a far cry from the sleeping beauty she was just a few minutes ago.

Grish sighs patiently. "Lily, I'd like to know what you did with my watch. Do you think you can get away with keeping it? Because if you do, you have another thing coming."

Confusion crosses her face at the mention of his watch, probably because she has a hundred more important things to worry about at that moment. But her eyes widen and her hand flies to the pocket in her dress.

"Here," she said chucking the watch at him. "I forgot all about it. I wasn't *stealing it*. People tend to forget things when they see a room full of massacred people and then are kidnapped, you know."

Grisha picks his watch up off the floor and snaps it back onto his wrist. "You need to calm down, woman."

Her head snaps back on her shoulders and she purses her lips. "Who do you think you are?" she screams, glaring at us.

I'm so not in the mood. "Lily, could you—"

But before I can finish my request, the vase on

the nightstand next to the bed comes flying in my direction.

Fuck all. I duck just in time for it to smash to pieces against the wall.

I look across the room at Valentin and nod. Reaching into my pocket, I pull out the zip ties I grabbed from the car's glove box—just in case— and toss him one.

"What are you doing?" she cries, retracting into the ball she was in a moment earlier. "Don't come near me with those things. I swear I'll—"

I grab one of her wrists and Val takes the other. In seconds, we flip Lily so she's face down, secured to the four-poster bed. Her legs, still free, thrash like a pissed-off wild animal. But at least she can't throw anything else.

"Lily," I say, "that was rude. We saved your life tonight."

More kicking, like a toddler having a tantrum. Which gives me an idea.

"You're being very naughty, Lily. It's time to teach you a lesson," I say, smoothing a hand over her lovely backside and finishing with a playful swat.

She stops kicking, and strains to look over her shoulder. "Don't you dare."

I shake my head. "Oh, I love a dare. Don't I, guys?" I ask Grisha and Valentin.

"You do at that, Artem," Val replies.

I gesture toward Grisha. He knows what I want without my saying a thing. He sits on the end of the bed and, gripping Lily's ankles, holds her legs down so she can no longer kick.

That doesn't mean she's suddenly submitting, though. And, to be honest, if she was, I'd be disappointed.

I take a seat on the bed next to her, and slowly slide her dress up to her thighs.

"Stop it," she wails, squirming as hard as she can.

"Sorry, Lily. It's time for you to learn a lesson," I say, slipping her dress up further, nearly to her waist, and exposing her lovely backside. I take the waistband of her panty hose and with a sharp tug, tear the nylon down the back seam so it splits in half and is easily pulled below her bottom. Now her ass is completely exposed, quivering and delicious and tempting as fuck, save for the thong panty wedged into her crack.

I run a hand over one of her cheeks and she flinches. But I continue to smooth her flesh, and she starts to relax. I move to the other cheek, also smooth and soft. And if I'm not mistaken, and not foolishly flattering myself, I catch the scent of her budding excitement.

Just what the doctor ordered.

Crack.

I bring my hand down on her left ass cheek when she least expects it, and she responds with a yelp. Without waiting for her to recover, I do it again. And again.

For a total of five times. Not so bad, really.

And then do the same on her right cheek.

By the time I finish, her breath is coming deep and raspy. And if feels like all my blood has rushed straight to my cock, leaving it about as hard as it's ever been.

Grisha and Valentin stare at her reddening bum with approval.

Her ass becomes a brilliant pink, brighter and brighter, even though I run my palm over it, soothing her burning flesh. She whimpers under me, unsure whether I am done with her punishment, or gearing up for another.

That's what makes this so much fun.

I can't tear my eyes away from her backside, so I straddle her legs and bend down to kiss her pretty behind. I gently part her cheeks and slide aside her thong to see her asshole, and as I do, she moans from embarrassment.

"Please don't," she whispers. "Please."

I lean over her, my lips next to her ear. "Do you think you can behave now? Do you think you can be a good girl? No throwing things, no thrashing around, no screaming? Do you think you can do that, Lily?" I murmur, rocking my hard-on against her ass through my trousers and reveling in her discomfort.

Fuck, how I want to pull my dick out and get some satisfaction. But there'll be time for that later.

"Y… yes. I will… behave," she whimpers. "Please, no more spanking. Please."

I take a knife from my pocket and slit one of the zip ties because she can't be completely trusted yet. "Such a beautiful girl," I croon, running my fingers through her hair, long since freed from the tidy knot it was in. "And such a good girl."

Grisha and Valentin peel off, leaving the two of us alone.

"I think you'll be comfortable here tonight, Lily. This really is a lovely room," I say, gesturing at the exquisitely outfitted digs that are now hers. I don't know how long she'll be with us, but she might as well be comfortable.

She looks around, really for the first time, and gives a slight nod. It's probably safe to assume her own home is not nearly this luxurious. Which is why I am glad we gave her this room. She deserves to be treated like a princess. I don't know much about her yet, but I have a feeling she's been over-looked, taken advantage of, and certainly under-appreciated. I want to change that for her, for at least as long as she's here, and beyond. Show her she deserves more. By the time we guys are done with her, she'll know her worth. If I have my way, she'll expect nothing less than what the world owes her and will demand it every day of her life.

I might not have wanted Valentin to bring her along, but I can't turn my back on a project.

"Have sweet dreams, Lily," I say, kissing her forehead.

But before I could leave her for the night, she grabs my arm with her free hand. "Artem?" she asks.

I sit on the edge of the bed again. "Yes? Are you okay?"

She looks down at her torn pantyhose, the thong that's covering what I'm sure is a pretty pussy, the dress that's pulled up nearly to her waist, and how one arm is still tied to the bed. "I… I was wondering if you would lay with me for a while. You know, just until I fall asleep. I… I know it sounds weird, but I think it will help."

Without a word, I remove what's left of her pantyhose, then release her tied hand and unzip her dress and pull it over her head. In her bra and panties, she's glorious.

How the fuck am I going to sleep with her and keep my hands to myself? Lucky for us both, I am exhausted.

I pull back the bed's fluffy down comforter and she slides under it. I remove my own clothes, down to my boxer shorts, and crawl in so I can wrap my arms around her. Sighing, she pushes back into me, and I bury my nose in her hair, clean and fresh, smelling of simple drugstore shampoo in spite of her long night of catering, gunfire, and blood.

Valentin might not have given much thought to what we're supposed to do with our lovely guest, but to my surprise, I am enjoying her. She's quite the Christmas present. Now it only she could enjoy herself too.

I may be able to help with that.

CHAPTER SIX

LILY

The windows are bolted shut.

So, no escaping that way.

I press my ear to the bedroom door. I'm not dressed yet, having woken up alone, still wearing my underwear. Seems that sometime during the night, after I'd finally fallen asleep, Artem bailed on me. Which is fine. Just because I wanted him to stay with me while I dozed off doesn't mean I wanted to wake up with him.

Criminals and kidnappers are not high on my list of people to hang out with. Even if they are freaking gorgeous hunks of masculinity. Damn them.

And as luck would have it—or wouldn't have it—the house beyond my bedroom door is full of the voices of my three abductors. So, I won't be walking out the front door, either.

I spot a robe at the bottom of my bed—clearly, someone was in here while I slept—and pull it on in case someone decides to pay me an unexpected visit. That's when I look around the room, really for the first time, since the night before when I'd been so distraught. And pissed off.

Not that I'm in that great of a mood right now. It's just that I'm not seconds away from absolutely losing my shit.

The room is surprisingly nice. Actually, more than nice. It's amazing. I had no idea kidnapping victims are afforded such nice digs.

The walls are painted in an eggshell-y white with a robin's egg blue wall just behind the bed. Long silky draperies are tied back from the windows, and there are two corners with over-stuffed reading chairs.

The bed itself, a four-poster canopy, is a work of art with sheer fabric draping across the top and down the posts, where it puddles on the floor. The bathroom is outfitted for a queen with a giant tub, stall with multiple shower heads, and marble on the floors and walls. At the far end is a vanity with a chair, and as I get closer, I find it covered with every high-end toiletry and makeup a girl could want. Seriously. This stuff is way better than anything I have at home. How did these things get here? Maybe they were left behind by the last prisoner?

And the whole place is spotlessly clean. Like eat off the floor clean.

It's awesome. And unsettling.

One look out the bathroom window, also secured with bars, tells me where I am. Approximately, anyway. I recognize the rolling hills and thick forests of Upstate New York. I have no idea how far outside the city we are since I passed out on the ride, but there aren't any other buildings for as far as I can see.

Wonderful. Not only have I been kidnapped but I am also in the middle of nowhere.

I finger the thick, plushy towels stacked on the bathroom shelves before I wander back to the bedroom. The irony of being surrounded by such luxury, while being a prisoner, makes me want to cry. Or laugh. Which one, I'm not sure.

Returning to my room, I plop down on the end of the bed, but immediately jump back to my feet with a shriek. I didn't realize that Artem's humiliating spanking would leave me so sore. Reaching under my robe, I find by butt cheeks still warm from his manhandling.

What was that all about, anyway, *spanking* me? These people are freaking crazy, not that I have any other criminal acquaintances to compare them to. Isn't it bad enough they're holding me prisoner? They have to beat my bare bottom too?

And when Artem sat on me, I knew very well he had a giant hard-on.

Damn pervert.

But was I any better?

I'd be lying if I didn't admit the act of having my bare butt exposed to the three men, as well as being punished in front of all of them, gave me a little bit of a tingle *down there*.

Okay, it wasn't a *little* tingle. It was *a lot* of tingle.

So this time, I lower myself to the bed carefully, spreading the soft robe under my bum for a smooth cushion, and run my hand over the bazil-lion-thread count sheets and duvet cover I snuggled in all night. I never before understood the appeal of fancy sheets, but after one night in such luxury, I think I might be a convert. This stuff is definitely *not* from Target.

Interestingly, on the other side of the room, my dress from the night before is neatly folded on top of a dresser, with my high heels just next to it. There's no sign of the trashed pantyhose.

Taking another look around, I spot a piece of paper taped to the closet door and cross the room to see what it is.

Merry Christmas. Please get dressed and join us as soon as you are ready.

A note from the guys?

And get dressed? In what? My blood-stained dress from the gallery? The robe I am currently wearing?

But when I wander over to my closet, the instructions make sense.

Hanging before me, in a walk-in closet nearly the size of my entire apartment, are several dresses, pairs of pants, blouses, and sweaters, which, after fingering, I realize are cashmere.

Freaking cashmere.

And they are my size.

What in god's name is going on here?

A knock at the door drives my heart into my throat. Had I locked it? And would it matter, anyway?

I glance around the closet, looking for a place to hide, and then realize that's about the dumbest thing to ever cross my mind.

Way to go, Lily!

"Um, hello?" I say with all the conviction I can muster.

"Hey, sleeping beauty, it's Christmas morning. Why don't you come join us?"

Is that Valentin? He sounds so much like his brother.

And what does he mean *join them*? In what? Singing Christmas carols? Baking cookies? Telling stories by the fire?

Somehow, I don't think these guys go to church.

"Sure. Be right there," I call.

Like I have anything else to do.

"It's already after noon, you know," he says.

Oh my god. Because I am phone-less, I have no idea I slept so long.

"Let me just get dressed then, okay?" I ask.

The footsteps move away, and I take a deep breath to calm myself. I rush into the bathroom and find I have a smudge of blood on my face from the night before, and there's mascara smeared under my eyes.

I turn the shower on hot and jump in, but not before locking the door.

"Well. Look what we have here."

I'm at the bottom of the stairs in what looks like a freaking mansion before Grisha notices me. I am being stealthy on purpose, and in fact listened from upstairs for as long as I could to see what the guys were up to.

They're watching Christmas Day football. Yup. My captors are actual football fans.

How has my life gotten so weird?

All three are now looking my way as I approach them in a room with a high-peaked ceiling, dark wood paneling, and crackly leather sofas and chairs. It even smells masculine, like someone sprayed something spicy-musky in the air. The fireplace, which covers almost an entire wall, holds a roaring fire, and as I draw near, Valentin gets up to add more wood to it. When he does, I see he has a gun on the table next to him and it's in a couple pieces. Is it broken? And why is it there, anyway?

Gone are the men's bespoke suits of the night before. But they hardly look casual. They're all wearing nice trousers with dress shirts tucked in, and Artem added a tweedy button-up vest for a stylish guy-in-the-country look.

Damn, they're hot. Even hotter than the night before.

And while they still look scary, only because I

know a little about who and what they are, I have a sense that they aren't lying when they say they plan to protect me.

The alternative flashes through my mind, but I push it away. I cross the room to join them, trying to act like spending Christmas Day imprisoned in a mansion wearing clothes someone else bought for me, with three gorgeous but dangerous men, is something that happens every day.

Nothing to see here, folks.

What if they hadn't dragged me along with them? If Sergey figures out I am a witness, will he really come after me?

I settle into one of the leather chairs. It's so soft and smells so good, I want to sit there all day. I smooth out the winter white slacks I found in my closet and pull down the cuffs of the matching silk blouse I selected, clothes that cost more than I make in a month. I check the loose bun I threw my damp hair into at the back of my neck because I didn't want to take the time to dry my hair, and in spite of everything, I feel pretty good about how I look, rocking my new Christmas Day outfit.

"Stunning. Just stunning," Artem says, nodding with approval.

I guess the right products and clothes make a difference.

He pours a glass of champagne and brings it over. I accept it because what else am I going to do?

But I just look at it.

And as if he can read my mind, he laughs lightly. "Don't worry, darling. We don't drug people. At least not very often."

The other guys laugh at this inside joke, and I take a sip of the champagne, because what the hell. It's not like I have anything else I need to do.

I look around the room with interest, pretending to check out their books and artwork, but really assessing the security situation, and hoping to identify an escape route. But I can't alert them to my thinking, so I smile pleasantly, and compliment the champagne.

"Hey, can I ask where are we? I fell asleep on the way here last night," I say breezily, faking small talk.

"Hudson Valley, honey," Grisha says.

Honey? I'm *honey*?

And I was right about our location.

"Do you always leave guns lying around?" I ask lightly, gesturing to the gun next to Valentin, like it was no big deal.

He raises his eyebrows. "Not normally. I'm just

cleaning this one." He pulls open the table's drawer and drops it inside.

There are probably guns all over the damn house.

"So Lily," he continues, "we have a Christmas present for you."

"What? You do? How? And how did you get these clothes for me?" I gesture to my outfit. I like the clothes, I can't deny it. A lot. But how they ended up in my closet is puzzling.

Valentin looks at the guys, who nod with satisfaction. "We know a lot of people, Lily. People who can take care of things for us, quickly and quietly. Speaking of," he says, getting up and crossing to the bar cart, "this is for you."

My mouth falls open and my stomach flutters.

No. Way.

No freaking way.

He presents me a robin's egg blue box from none other than Tiffany. *Tiffany.* One of the famous blue boxes, all tied up with a pretty white satin ribbon.

For *me*.

I take it slowly, not wanting to come off as greedy, and hold it, weighing it, and admiring it. The box on its own is perfection. I mean, even if it is empty, like some sort of mean joke, I don't think I'd care.

But it's not empty.

I jiggle it around to savor the treat and for a split-second consider not opening it, maybe *never* opening it, instead hanging on to it like it's a mysterious treasure, too precious to see the light of day.

I mean, it's not like I'm ever going to get anything from Tiffany again.

And what's with a Christmas gift from these guys, anyway? Is this a thing among certain kidnappers?

But when it comes down to it, I don't give a damn. I want my Tiffany present. So, I tear the box open like a hungry little animal.

I gasp, and my hands begin to tremble. "Oh my god. This is incredible," I say, pulling out a diamond bangle bracelet.

A *diamond bracelet*. For *me*.

I've never gotten anything from Tiffany. I've never even held anything from Tiffany. In fact, I've never even been *close* to anything from Tiffany, that is, no closer than peering into their display windows, like a less fancy Holly Golightly.

I roll the bangle in my fingers, feelings its weight—not just its physical weight, but the implication, the aura of it. I know it's expensive. I know it's prestigious.

I also know the guys are trying to buy me in some way, for some reason. And I don't understand why.

I shouldn't accept it. It will somehow put me in debt to them. But it's so pretty. So, so pretty.

I'll just try it on.

I slide on the bangle and as I knew it would be, it's perfection rolled into a few ounces of metal and stone. Extending my wrist, I show the guys. I say nothing, because I just don't know what to say.

A measly *thank you* might insult the moment.

And then, when I know perfectly well that I should take it back off, return it to the box, explain it's inappropriate, and say *thank you anyway*, I continue to admire it on my wrist.

CHAPTER SEVEN

GRISHA

I KNEW she'd love the bracelet.

We all did.

First of all, what woman doesn't love a little trinket from Tiffany? And this woman in particular, one who clearly lives a relatively austere, workaholic life, would never expect that such a gift would come her way. It's not like she doesn't deserve it, oh, fuck no. She deserves it more than nearly anyone we know. The thing is, she doesn't *know* she deserves it. But as she sticks around with us longer, she'll understand. She's deserving of this, and more, for exactly the reason she doesn't believe it.

I love a work in progress, a challenge. I want to spoil this woman precisely because I know she'll never *be* spoiled. She'll never take pretty things for granted, come to expect them, or feel entitled.

Appreciation spreads across her face as she looks from one of us guys to the next. It almost makes me want to cry.

And I don't cry.

The happiness that's replaced the weary, suspicious look on her face, for however long it happens to last, is worth all the trouble of the fucked-up night before. Including how she got her bottom beaten.

For a moment, I'm not bothered by how Sergey got away.

It's Christmas, and we have a beautiful woman in the house. Sure, she's here against her will, but she'll come to understand this is the only place she's safe—with Valentin, Grisha, and myself by her side.

"How did you... where did you get this?" she asks when she's recovered a little.

I decide to be straight with her. "We have a personal shopper at Tiffany, as well as at some other places. They deliver whenever we need them to. Even if it's the middle of the night."

She wrinkles her brow. "Really? That's a thing?"

Artem shrugs. "You spend enough money and all the world's *no's* suddenly turn to *yes's.*"

She sits back in her chair sipping her champagne, considering Artem's words. Surely, she knows this is how the world works, given the business she's in.

But that doesn't matter, and if I have my way, I'll keep her innocent, just like she is, indefinitely. Although hanging out with us has probably put a time limit on her naiveté.

I reach for her hand, which she tentatively gives me. "I could use some help in the kitchen. Are you game?" I ask.

Her eyes open wide. "Sure. Yeah. I love cooking."

"Well, come with me then," I say, leading the way.

A chef brought most of our Christmas meal, so there isn't much for us to do, but what little there is left, like heating things up, I want Lily's help with.

"This is incredible," she breathes, looking around in awe at our state-of-the-art chef's kitchen.

Artem had insisted on it when we got the place. He's the primary cook of the three of us. In fact, it's probably just a matter of minutes until he joins us in the kitchen to make sure we aren't screwing up the chef's creations.

"It is nice, isn't it?" I say. Almost nice enough to make me forget the pressures of my work.

But nothing can make that completely go away.

Except for maybe some female company.

"Okay, Lily. Here is your task. Chef made these pie crusts, so we just need to put the apples in them and the crust on top."

Her face brightens and life feels almost normal for a second. "Great. Do you have a peeler?" she asks, rolling up the sleeves of her silk blouse.

I toss her an apron and we get down to business. It's strangely domestic considering... everything, but also nice to get my head out of the world I usually live in.

And while Lily works away, I'm mostly pretending to be industrious to have the chance to watch her. She bites her lips in concentration, ensuring every last piece of apple skin is gone from the fruit, then cutting the slices in perfect, uniform sizes. It's funny to see someone take so much care with something so mundane.

Amazing too. I'm so immersed in the crazy world the guys and I exist in that I forget women like Lily even exist. And as she peels and peels, small red tendrils of hair slip from the messy bunching at the back of her neck, clinging to her slightly sweaty skin.

Holy fuck, I'm hard.

As per Chef's instruction, Lily adds sugar and cinnamon, then loads it all into the pie dish. Her hands are covered with pie goop, and goddamn, I want a taste.

She pinches the corners of the crust closed and dessert is ready for the oven. But before she can do anything else, I take her wrists.

Actually, it's more like I seize them.

She gasps, her fear of the night before returning to her face.

And this makes me even harder.

Yeah, I'm a dick that way.

"Look how messy your hands are, pretty girl," I say, looking between her wide blue eyes and her coated hands. "We can't let you mess up your new clothes now, can we?"

She realizes I'm playing, and her shoulders drop. "You're right," she flirts, "and I'd be broken-hearted if I did anything to this amazing outfit."

I take a step closer. "I'm here to help, in any way I can," I say quietly, taking her first finger into my mouth and cleaning it of the delicious apple pie concoction.

I take a finger from her other hand and do the

same, and with a mouthful of sweetness bring my lips to her unadorned earlobe, making a mental note to pick up earrings to match her new bracelet.

She stiffens as I close my lips on her soft skin, so I pull back and look at her, really look at her. She's biting her bottom lip as if to bleed off the pleasure I'm giving her, so I swipe my tongue across her mouth and step back.

"Let's get your hands clean," I say as she stands there like she wants more.

Which is exactly the plan.

I stand behind her, my hands reaching around her waist to the warm water running from the spigot before her. I begin to wash away the stickiness left from the apple pie and as I do, I bury my nose in her hair, still damp from her shower, smelling clean and fresh, just like she does.

I continue to hold her hands under the warm spray. When my lips find her neck, she releases a long exhale, her head dropping forward. Her fingers grab mine in reflex. With my front pressed against her back, there's no question she's fully aware of my hard cock, and the way it is announcing my desire for her.

"You're fucking beautiful, you know that, right?" I whisper.

Her head lolls to one side. "Th… thank you, Grisha."

She says my name slowly, drawing out the syllables, and I think about how a long stroke of my cock in her pussy might feel.

Continuing to press her against the sink, I grab a towel and dry both our hands, then proceed to slowly unbutton her blouse. Once open, I take her bare breasts in my hands, stroking and kneading, while rocking my hard dick against her. My hands wander to the waistband of her pants, which I have open in seconds.

All while her breath comes harder and the guys in the next room yell at the TV.

I reach inside her panties, between her bare pussy lips, and find, to my delight, she's not just wet but soaked. As I run my fingers through her cleft, she shudders and sighs, pressing her ass back against me.

"I'm going to fuck you now, darling," I murmur in her ear.

Before I can do anything else, she hooks her fingers in the waistband of her pants and with a shove, drops them to the floor. With her dressed in nothing but her unbuttoned blouse, now falling off her shoulders, I bend her forward with one hand while pulling my cock out of my trousers with the other.

Reaching around to play with her clit, I position myself at her opening and gently pulse. "How are you feeling, baby?" I whisper.

Without a word, she reaches back and puts a hand on my now-bare hip. She digs her fingers into my flesh and pulls me closer until I begin to enter her, and my god, it's heaven. Pure heaven. I'm barely inside and her pussy is creamy and soft, just like the silk blouse now puddling on the floor at our feet.

"Goddamn, you feel nice," I say, and with a savage grunt, push all the way inside her until my balls are slapping her ass and she's moaning in satisfaction.

I knew she had an itch to be scratched. It was written all over her face. This serious, steadfast girl has gone way too long with no outlet for her true nature.

I slide in and out, the tension in my balls nearly unbearable, and her moans tell me she's getting close. I take my fingers off her clit and shove them into the hair gathered at her neck. I push her head down, nearly into the sink, raising her ass so I can fuck her faster and harder.

And I do.

She clenches around my dick and begins to shudder, her hands on the kitchen counter for balance. Her moans are sweet and make me think of the sugar and cinnamon I licked off her fingers and all I know is that I want this to last forever. I barely know this woman but I want more of her, so much more. Maybe too much.

In my last lucid thought before exploding, I tell myself not to be such an idiot over a woman I just met, and then my cum travels like the water through a goddamn firehose. Right before I start to spurt, I pull out of Lily and come down the crack of her pretty ass.

Goddamn, I'm in trouble.

CHAPTER EIGHT

LILY

The apple pie's done.

Thank goodness for kitchen timers. If this one hadn't buzzed, I might still be draped over the kitchen sink with Grisha's cum running down my butt crack, the pie turning into a flammable brick of char.

I don't know what the hell has come over me. Maybe a brush with death does this to a person, where you throw caution to the wind. It makes absolutely no sense, but I can't resist these guys.

And they're my captors.

But, at least for the time being, I'm not going to think too hard about it. What good has worrying ever done me anyway, aside from turning me into a boss-pleasing, perfectionist workaholic?

Grisha unexpectedly helps me cleans me up with a dishtowel and lends a hand in pulling my clothes back on. He, however, still has his pants around his ankles and he doesn't seem bothered by it, at all. Guess that's a guy thing.

"Well, well, well," Valentin laughs, leaning against the kitchen doorway like a model from a Ralph Lauren ad.

These damn guys.

"I see my big brother wasted no time getting to know our lovely houseguest," he says as I finish buttoning my blouse.

Should I be embarrassed? Ashamed? Guilty?

Because I am none of these. Something about what just happened sort of flicked a switch in me. Okay, maybe not as dramatic as all that, but I realize I have some power in this situation. I can make the best of things.

I mean, if I'm going to be a prisoner, I might as well be in a beautiful house with gorgeous clothes and the three most handsome men I've ever laid eyes on.

One of whom, by the way, can fuck like a champ. Are the others equally as talented?

Holy crap. They've turned me into a monster.

"Oh, hi Val," I say cheerfully, like people walk in on me all the time, post-sex. "Can you grab the pie from the oven?" I ask, wiping down the kitchen counter like it's the most important job in the world and I'm the only person who can do it correctly.

I have a sudden urge to look busy. Maybe it's from all my years of managing parties.

But Valentin doesn't move.

"What's wrong?" I ask, eyebrows raised like I own the place.

He looks like he doesn't even know where the oven is.

Grisha laughs and grabs two thick dishtowels. "You don't want to ask my brother to do *anything* in the kitchen, Lily. The man can hardly boil water."

I turn and look Valentin up and down, and gather all my confidence. Which isn't saying much, but still. "Geez. I thought you might be more useful than that," I say in my best, new sassy tone.

Holy crap, am I getting salty.

And my saltiness is not lost on Valentin. "I can be useful in many other ways, if you'd like me to show you at some point," he says, his voice taking on a new-to-me deep, scratchy tone.

Holy shit. Do I have a little flirtation going on?

I respond by flipping my hair over my shoulder and giving him my best seductive smile. This might not be natural for me, but I've seen a few things in my line of work and while I don't take written notes, I sure as shit commit a lot of my observations to memory.

Especially how women get men to eat out of their hands.

I never imagined putting this stuff to use—I watch mostly out of curiosity—but maybe some of my long, thankless hours watching rich people party are beginning to pay off.

Satisfied the kitchen counter is clean enough to eat off of, and that Grisha rescued the pie from the oven in the nick of time, I sashay out of the kitchen to head to my room for fresh clothes.

I brush up against Valentin, mainly because I can. "I'll get back to you on that, Val."

A few hours later, after an incredible Christmas dinner of oysters, salmon medallions, filet mignon, and assorted exotic vegetables and sauces, we're sitting around the dinner table ready to explode. The room is warm from the roaring fire, we're drinking some incredible wine, and we're all a little drowsy.

Well, to be honest, *I'm* not. I took only a sip or two of wine and a few bites of dinner, not wanting to burst the buttons of my second pair of pants for the day. But most importantly, I'm biding my time, listening carefully to gather anything I can about the situation I'm in. All I know so far is something I overheard about *a bratva*.

Or maybe it's *the* bratva. I'm not sure. I've never heard the word. But it seems tied into the guys' Russian names. I'd Google it if I had my damn phone.

"Gentlemen," I start, hoping to catch them off guard, "when are you planning on telling me what's up with Sergey, and what's behind everything that went down last night?" I am cool. Casual. As if I'm asking about tomorrow's weather.

I hoping the wine will loosen their tongues a bit.

They look at each other for a minute, I suppose communicating in their silent criminal-kidnapper language, and turn back to me.

Artem leans onto the dining room table with his elbows and rubs the sexy facial scruff on his chin.

Wow. They're actually considering my inquiry.

"Sergey's gallery… takes care of large amounts of cash for us. Unfortunately for him, he's been helping himself to more than his share of it," he says.

My mind races with more questions than I can spit out. But I do have one big one.

"Why don't you just put the money in the bank? You know, protect it? Then you don't have to depend on someone like Sergey."

There. Solved it.

Or not. The room gets so quiet, you can hear a pin drop. All eyes are on me.

And looking at me like I'm a complete freaking idiot. I clearly missed the memo on something.

Valentin takes a deep breath, like I'm trying his last ounce of patience. This may be the last of my nosy questions. "Lily, when you have the kind of businesses we do, which generate large amounts of cash—and I mean *really* large—putting the money in the bank attracts... unwanted attention."

"I don't understand," I say before I grasp that I really need to shut the hell up. "I work with a lot of cash businesses like caterers, florists, and lighting companies through the party planning company. They don't do that."

Valentin considers my question. "I get that, but I'm talking about large sums of money. Like more money than these businesses ever see in their lifetimes."

He reaches across the table to top off my wine

without noticing I'd only taken a few sips of it anyway.

"Wh… what sort of business generates that much cash?" I ask in a small voice.

God I need to shut up.

He stares at me.

And the hairs on the back of my neck stand.

"Our lovely guest sure has a lot of questions, doesn't she?" Artem says, smiling. "Look, Lily. The cash flows through Sergey's gallery—well, it was flowing through his gallery until we realized he was skimming—and he makes up fake bills of sale for obscenely expensive paintings." He sits back in his seat. "Everyone's happy."

I swallow. "And he would be after me because I saw him try to kill you guys?"

He nodded slowly, satisfied I was finally getting it.

"Do you… do you think he knows who I am? What my name is?" I ask in a shaking voice. This is not good. In fact, it's very bad. And I don't mean just for myself. What about my sisters Charleigh and Evie? Do I need to be concerned about them? Or will they be okay because they're clear across the country?

And then there's my father. But I'm not really worried about him.

He nods again. "Probably. I mean, he hired your company for the party, right? He can find out exactly who you are."

Now it's my turn to nod. "Yeah. But I'm a nobody. I don't know why he would care about me."

Valentin scoots his chair over and throws an arm around my shoulder. "We will be neutralizing him soon. Don't worry, baby. We won't let anything happen to you."

Neutralize. Oh god.

"What about my job? I have to get back to work. How long will I be here? How long will this… neutralizing take?"

I look around. This 'safe house' is sweet, no doubt, and my bedroom is fit for a movie star. But it wasn't exactly my idea to come here. I have my own place, for which I pay an exorbitant amount of rent. Therefore, this girl needs to work.

"Don't know," he says with a shrug. "But we'll be contacting your boss to let her know you'll be out for a while."

What?

Oh, hell no. They don't know my boss. She's a grade-A bitch, and regardless of how hard I've worked for her, she won't think twice about firing me. It's one thing that I am being kept in this place against my will, but another that my job should be jeopardized. Unless the guys plan on never letting me go…

My stomach drops.

No. No way.

But, one thing at a time. I take a deep breath. The first thing is to stay safe from Sergey. And I have the guys to help with that.

At least, that's what they're promising.

Then, I can worry about next steps.

Merry fucking Christmas I think, twirling my new bracelet around my wrist.

SUDDENLY, to my surprise, we're back in New York City, the very place I thought we were supposed to be avoiding. But the guys promise they have someone tailing Sergey, and that everything will be fine.

It's not like I have much say in the matter, anyway.

After an afternoon of trying on clothes at the very Christmas-y Bergdorf Goodman, a store I've been inside of only once, where I'd splurged on a lipstick just to buy one little thing there, we head downtown to a restaurant I've never heard of, which the guys are raving about. I have no complaints, if I really think about it. I have a couple shopping bags of new things and am about to get another free meal with three good-looking men. What the hell, it's the Christmas season.

I'm getting really good at looking at the bright side of things.

For example, the ride from the Hudson Valley to the city takes two hours. Do you think I sat in the backseat of the stretch limo the whole way, looking out the window?

No. No, I did not.

Since my Christmas Day encounter in the kitchen with Grisha, I've wanted more. Lots more. Yet I'm really not sure how to approach the guys. Strangely, they haven't initiated anything... sexy. Which is strange. So, I lay in bed last night, taking care of business, all by myself. Their indifference toward me, even though they're perfectly polite, is driving me crazy.

Maybe it's designed to do that. If so, it's working.

For our day in the city, I'm wearing a short, lacy, fitted dress with high heels. And it just so happens, my hem rises as I sit, exposing a nice swath of leg.

And the band of my thigh-high stockings.

This does not go unnoticed.

I run my fingertips along my hem and fake-bashfully shimmy my dress down in a pretend attempt at modesty. But Artem can't stop staring, which is kind of the point. At the other end of the limo, the brothers are deep in conversation about one thing or another. But I'll have their attention soon.

With Artem on the bench seat opposite me, I cross and uncross my legs very slowly, absent-mindedly leaving my knees parted for longer than I need to. When he gets a flash of my nude panties and what lies below them, a corner of his mouth twitches up in a smile, and his gaze rises to meet mine.

When he sees me staring back at him, the other corner of his mouth curls to meet the first, and his sexy smile washes over me like a thousand teasing pin pricks. He gestures toward my crossed knees with his chin while waving his fingers from side to side.

I get the message.

So, I open my knees a bit more.

Again, he waves his fingers from side to side.

Biting my lower lip, I look toward the other end of the limo, where Grisha and Valentin remain deep in conversation. I turn back to Artem and part my knees a good three or four inches, enough to see my pussy through my panties. The goods are still obscured by shadows, though.

So, he waves his hand again. *Spread them more.*

But this time, I wrinkle my brow, like I don't understand.

He raises his eyes as if to say *watch yourself, young lady.*

And that's all I need. Blood rushes to my core, and a heavy throb begins to build in the very spot where Artem's gaze is glued. I've never thought of myself as an exhibitionist, but I want Artem to *see* me. I want them all to *see* me. I am tired of being invisible, unremarkable, and always so damn dutiful. I want to do something wicked to show these guys that I can, that I'm not a goody two-shoes, but rather a passionate woman with needs.

And I guess I also want to show *myself* that I can, that I'm more than some boring-ass wage slave who has nothing going on in her life besides her job.

So I part my legs more, and with my hands on my hem, slide my dress up until the V of my panties peeks out. I feel so sexy. I *am* so sexy. And powerful.

Like I can do anything.

Valentin, glancing our way, does a double take

and stops talking. Grisha follows his gaze, and they grin.

Bingo. I've got them.

I book limos for parties all the time, but I've never been in one. I've always wondered what went on in them since they are essentially parties on wheels. With a window separating the driver from the back, you can do whatever you want, I figure.

I am ready to give it a shot.

The brothers scoot down to our end of the car, flanking Artem, who gets up and moves to sit next to me. Pressing his lips to mine, I fall into him as he runs a warm, large hand up my inner thigh.

When his fingers land on my pussy, it's all I can do to hold still and not push into him to increase his pressure, like the greedy girl I am. With the brothers sitting opposite me, Artem pulls my legs further open to give them a show. I'm happy to oblige.

"Take my cock out," he demands.

As I reach for his fly, his fingers slip inside the leg of my panties, pulling the crotch aside and exposing my excited flesh to the cool air of the limo. It's exhilarating, his touching me with the others watching, and I finally allow myself to squirm into his touch, because I need it. Badly.

And when he plunges his fingers inside me, my entire body clenches, including the fist I have around his cock.

"Fuck, baby, stroke me like that," he growls quietly.

The rolling of the limo on the freeway adds to our movement and I gasp, making no other sound, while an orgasm rocks me. I push so hard on Artem's hand for more pressure I wonder if I might break his wrist, and I don't even care. I'm a rutting animal, driven by nothing more than instinct, a dangerous desire that I know could very well be the end of me.

CHAPTER NINE

VALENTIN

WE ARE FUCKED.

So very fucked.

When we dragged Lily out of Sergey's gallery on Christmas Eve—or should I say, when *I* dragged her out, since it was my idea—I had no end game in mind. I hadn't thought through what the hell we were going to do with her. Where we'd take her. How long we'd keep her. Not even what we'd *tell* her. None of that. I was all adrenaline and instinct, which tends to crowd out the details, the fine print, the ability to see beyond a moment in time.

Which, when it comes down to it, is what kept

us three guys, and Lily, alive. The simple fact is that we were her only chance at survival, and I wanted to protect her from that asshole Sergey who, if I know him at all, would have come after her with a vengeance. The man's a loser, but he also knows how to tie up a loose end.

And Lily is a loose end. A big one, to be honest.

But through it all—scooping her up like I did and whisking her away before Sergey could sink a bullet into her head—there *was* an unacknowledged notion spinning around the back of my brain. I can't deny it, now that a couple days have passed and the adrenaline rush has subsided.

I want to know more about her. Actually, I want to know *everything* about her. What makes her laugh, cry, come, get angry. All of it.

Hell if that's not a bizarre reaction to someone I'd only seen pour shrimp cocktail on my friend.

So, with no plan other than to get her the hell out of Manhattan, we dragged her up to the Hudson Valley to one of our safe houses, with no thought about what was next. Pretty fucking out of character for me and to a lesser extent, Artem and Grisha. We usually walk into new situations with eyes wide open. A decent plan laid out. An idea of what we want our end game to look like.

But the last day or so, I've been thinking about

what's next for us. I mean, we can't keep her for-fucking-ever, right?

Or can we?

And now look at us. Smitten like three goddamn pussy lovesick teenagers.

Love. Yeah, I said love.

I don't know if I love her, but fuck, I like her. Like I want her *to stick around for a long time,* like her.

She's the kind of woman every smart man wants. Beautiful, intelligent, independent, smart-assed, and a goddamn animal in the sack.

Seriously. This woman can tire all of us and still be up for more, as evidenced by our limo ride to the city.

And now here we are at dinner, at a chi-chi Tribeca restaurant that's decorate to the nines in all manner of holiday ornamentation, and all I can do is fucking stare, my gaze drawn to her like a magnet while she absently sips the wine my brother ordered and glances over the menu. The glass she sets down has the slight imprint of her red lipstick on the rim, and all I can think is how during the limo ride here, those lips were wrapped around my cock, and remained so until I exploded down our pretty girl's throat. God bless Artem for initiating car sex.

It's one of my weaknesses, and now, apparently, it's one of Lily's too.

Her stunning red hair—long and thick, sometimes straight and sometimes wavy because she likes to mix it up—is something I can barely keep my fingers out of. But the thing about her that gets me the most are her plump lips, which are nearly always bright red, a perfect contrast to her pale complexion.

It is not lost on me that she also draws the gaze of every other man in the restaurant. Some, who are with women, are appropriately discreet. Others stare as carelessly as they want, turning away only when I give them my *fuck off* look.

Works like a charm.

And through all of this, the lovely Lily is blissfully unaware. The woman could cause a car wreck just crossing the street and keep walking on her merry way because she has no freaking idea she impacts men like she does.

She excuses herself for the ladies' room and her momentary absence takes the wind out of our sails. The table gets quiet aside from cutlery clinking on our plates, and we chew our food and drink our wine, pouring more when a glass gets low. Whoever would have thought that some woman could do this to the three of us guys?

Without even trying?

We've been around the block. We don't just fall all over hot babes. I mean we *did*, in the past, sure, when we were younger. Like a truck without brakes careening down a steep hill, back when the hormones were completely fucking out of control.

Not that it's that different now.

I need to get her out of my head. We have businesses to run, and don't need to be distracted by a pretty girl. Shit like this has been the downfall of many a man, going all the way back to Adam and Eve. I've worked too hard to get to where I am, and nothing is going to mess with that, no matter how badly I want to fuck someone.

Finally, Grisha breaks the silence. "Guys, I got a text a few minutes ago that someone in the cell has located Sergey. Didn't want to bring it up in front of Lily. Apparently, he's cooling his heels in Southern California, thinking no one will ever find him there."

Christ, the man's a dumbfuck. "I can't believe he's unaware that our reach includes the *entire* United States. Anyway, what's the status?" I ask.

"He should go down today or tonight. Remember, it's three hours earlier there," Grisha says.

The next question I want to ask is one I'm sure is on each of our minds.

"After he's gone, is Lily is safe? Do we think the risk to her will be eliminated?" I ask. Sergey's exit from this world doesn't guarantee anything, a fact we should never forget.

Artem rubs his hand over his face. "You know everyone is linked in this business. Sergey may have set up a contingency plan, knowing his life is on the line, and that could leave her in just as much danger after he's gone as before."

She's not going to be happy to hear that.

In one regard, I wish Lily hadn't been pulled into our lives. As much as I like her—no, actually, crave her—things would be simpler for her if nothing had happened at the gallery that night. She could have gone home and woken up the next day to carry on with her usual routine, as unsatisfying as it may have been.

But she was in the wrong place at the wrong time, and that's thrown a wrench into her life. Not that we are obligated, but we have worked to make her time under our watch as comfortable as possible. But when it comes down to it, I imagine she'd probably rather not be stuck with us, no matter how we spoil and pamper her.

And fuck her.

Of course, I hope I'm wrong. I hope she can reconcile what she's given up with what she has now. Freedom is not all it's cracked up to be. Her life before us did not sound all that fabulous, from what I know.

Still, no one wants to be told when then can come and go. And I hope we can change that, in due time.

Artem looks at the full plate of food in front of Lily's place at the table. Untouched, and growing cold. "Uh, guys, Lily's still gone. No one takes that long in the ladies' room."

He jumps out of his seat and hustles toward the ladies' room, fingering the waistband of his pants to check his gun.

"You wait here, Grish," I say to my brother, jumping up to follow Artem, hoping to attract as little attention as possible.

I catch up to him at the door to the ladies' room. We draw our guns. With a nod at each other, we shove open the door in one fast and violent movement.

"Oh my god. *Help me*," Lily cries the moment she sees us.

With a gun pointed at Lily's temple, a woman with long black hair and a harsh face whips around to see who's interfering with her attempts to steer our girl out of the restaurant.

So much for hoping Lily's safe with Sergey out

of the picture. Artem is right, the fucker does have an extensive and loyal network. But our network is bigger, stronger, and undoubtedly more highly skilled.

With the woman distracted, now focusing on Artem, I catch her off guard and knock her arm away from Lily. She stumbles off balance and throws a punch my way. She's well trained, I'll give her that, but still no match for me. I catch her arm and pin it between two of mine, applying pressure.

When I hear a *snap*, I know with confidence that she's out of commission.

She groans, stifling anything louder, and looks at her arm, now bent at an unnatural angle.

"Sorry, lady. If you go to the ER, they'll set that for you. Should only take six weeks or so to heal," Artem says. "'Course, they'll also ask you a lot of questions."

I chuckle. Can't help myself. The woman's face pales from the pain she's in, and even more so knowing there isn't much she can do about it. Sergey might have hired her, but now that she's failed her mission, he'll drop her like a hot rock.

She is screwed.

And she knows it.

"Fuck you," she spits. "And you too, you bitch," she says to Lily.

Artem takes the woman's good arm and twists it up behind her back. "I'll take care of this delightful woman, Val. You take Lily back to the table."

Artem leads the woman out of the ladies' room and turns left, which I know will take him through the kitchen and out the back door. I'm pretty sure there's someone out back waiting for her, and that Artem plans to straighten them both out.

So to speak.

Threat neutralized, I turn back to Lily. Her eyes are wide, kind of comatose actually, and as soon as I put a hand on her arm to comfort her, she turns to the bathroom sink and gets sick.

I'm not surprised. Just unhappy this had to happen, that Lily had to see this, experience this, be part of this.

As much as I want her in my life—all our lives, I should say—she doesn't deserve this sort of terror. But I can protect her. It's the most important thing I can do. And, really, the *only* thing I can do.

After splashing water on her face, Lily crumbles into my arms. "How… how did they find me? Why were they waiting for me?" she cries. "Is this ever going to end?"

She buries her face in my chest, shaking from the confrontation. I don't blame her. My adrenaline is running fast and furious too. Artem and I got to Lily just in time. If we'd waited much longer, Lily might be gone. Sure, we'd find her, eventually. But she might not be alive.

"Take a deep breath, sweetie. You're safe now," I say, pulling her off my chest so I can look at her, my hands on either side of her face.

"H… how can I be?" she asks.

"Hey. What's going on?"

We whip around to see who's joining us, and in the process, I draw my gun again.

But it's just my brother.

"Grish. One of Sergey's cronies had a gun to Lily's head and was about to show her out of the restaurant."

And probably land a bullet right between her eyes.

He runs his hands through his hair. "Well, that would be a waste of an expensive dinner," he jokes. "Holy fuck." He reaches for Lily and draws her into his arms just like I did.

She needs to know we all have her back.

"What did Artem do with the shooter?" he asks.

"He escorted her out. Right after breaking her arm."

Lily gasps, then turns again for the bathroom sink.

Christ almighty.

Grisha lets out a long exhale of air when he realizes the shape Lily's in. "Well, just got word, like one minute ago, that our people have Sergey. So, his time on Earth has just been reduced to minutes. His cronies will all scatter to the wind now, including the woman whose arm you just broke. Not only is she not gonna get paid for this, she has to look for a new boss. After her arm heals, that is."

Lily is slumping at the sink, and Grisha catches her just before she passes out.

"We've got to get her the hell out of here."

Just then, the bathroom door bursts open, and two women walk in. 'Course they stop short when they see Grisha and me.

I step toward them so they can't enter any further. "Apologies, ladies. Our friend here just got… sick. We're taking her home right now."

Their eyes widen and they back out the door with murmurs of *certainly, I'm so sorry,* and *feel better honey.*

Lily perks up at the new voices and realizes, just like we have, that she needs to get home.

"Can you walk, darlin'?" Grisha asks. "Val and I can each take one of your arms."

She looks between the two of us, trying to

muster a hopeful expression, and nods. In spite of all that just went down, she's still put together. Her hair's a little mussed, and there's some black mascara under her eyes, but nothing worse than that.

Amazing.

"I'm safe now?" she whispers, leaning into us both.

I'm pretty sure she's going to be fine. But I know better than to make promises.

On the way home, we're mostly quiet in the limo. I'm sitting right next to Lily with my arms around her. She's trying to act tough, but she gives herself away as she continues to tremble and wipe at the occasional tear.

On the night of the gallery party, we'd intended to take out Sergey for our own purposes. It was business and nothing more. But I now realize that in the period of a few short days, it has become personal too.

If anything happens to Lily, I… well, I don't know what the fuck I'll do. I haven't met anyone like her in a long time, if ever, and I'm not about to let her slip through my fingers. Not now. Not ever.

At least not if I can help it.

CHAPTER TEN

LILY

WHEN WE FINALLY GET BACK TO the safe house after what should have been a nice day in the city followed by dinner, I head straight to my room. I don't want to talk. I only want to take a hot shower, get in bed, and try and figure out how my life has gotten so fucked up.

But the truth is, if it wasn't for the guys saving me that night in Sergey's gallery, I'd be as dead as all those other people on the floor. Sergey would have murdered me just like he did everyone else.

And that would be that.

My boss would send her regrets to my dad and

sisters, explaining that New York was a dangerous place. She'd take no blame at all.

The other girls in the company would freak, and most of them would probably quit. Several would leave New York altogether, running back to the safety of the towns they'd come from. Maybe one or two would stick around, at the mercy of our cold-hearted boss, who'd throw them to the wolves without a morsel of concern. After all, the woman 'has a company to run.'

So maybe falling into the lives of these guys isn't the worst thing that could happen. I'm alive, for cripes' sake. That's a plus. Question is, what the hell is my life supposed to look like, going forward? What kind of life can I even have?

My mind swirls with these questions, and more, until I am dizzy. Am I doomed to a screwed-up life of running and hiding? Or am I on the precipice of something new? Maybe exciting? All I know, or at least suspect, is that going back to where I was before is looking less and less likely. And less and less appealing, when it comes down to it.

Before I get to my room, Artem calls after me.

I suppose I should have said goodnight. And thanked them for saving my life.

Is this the sort of thing I need to get used to?

"Hey darlin', I know you're tired, but can you join us for a moment?" he asks.

Of course. I owe them at least that much. I might be tired and cranky, but they don't deserve my crappy mood.

I return to the living room, where I curl up into a huge chair. With my arms crossed and my legs tucked under me, I feel like a turtle in her shell, as safe as I can make myself from danger.

But the truth is, I'm just as vulnerable as I've ever been. Sergey may be gone, but there's always another one like him right around the corner.

And as if he's reading my mind, Artem addresses my concerns.

"You are safe as long as you are with us, Lily. I know that might not be the news you want to hear. But your old life is a thing of the past."

A lump builds in my throat, but why? It's not like Artem is telling me anything I don't already know.

And why exactly would I want to go back to my old life? All I did was work. Watch other people have fun. I am the very definition of a wallflower.

So. Freaking. Pathetic.

Why have I been satisfied with that for so long? How could I be? Life was happening all around me. I was being left behind.

Maybe what I had was enough at the time, because I was finally free of my toxic father, who's been telling me for as long as I can remember that I'm lazy and dumb and will never amount to anything. Is that why I've lived the way I have? To prove to him or myself that I *can* do something, and do it well?

"I… I know you *say* I'm safe," I blurt out in a trembling voice. "At least for the time being. But the question is, what will things look like for me going forward?"

I'm not sure anyone can answer that. But I've got to ask.

"We don't know that yet. No one does. But whatever you decide to do, Lily, we will offer you protection. You will need it. But we do hope," Valentin pauses, looking at his brother and Artem, "that you'll consider staying with us."

"*Stay?*"

I'm not sure what that means.

Actually, I'm not sure of anything at the moment. It's late, I'm exhausted, and no surprise, I've got a massive headache looming.

"Yeah. Stay," Grisha repeats.

I can't lie. I do feel something for these guys, and it goes beyond the crazy passion I have for them. But do they *really* want me? Or am I just their project of the month?

Grisha beckons me over, and I settle into his lap with my head against his chest. God, it feels good. It feels like where I *belong*.

I think these guys do want me. I can feel it. I am important to them.

But that doesn't mean everything's settled. I need more than that.

"I… care for you. All of you." *Care.* What an inadequate word. "Probably more than you know, and probably more than I want to admit to myself. But I can't hide out in this house for the rest of my life and be happy. I want to work. I want to have a life. Go places, experience things."

And have the love of three wonderful men. But I wasn't ready to say that. It was much too scary. Risky.

Grisha strokes my hair, long since having fallen out of the neat bun I'd twisted it into earlier that day.

"You can do that, baby. You aren't trapped in this house or anywhere else. You'll just need a bodyguard. Someone discreet, who no one will notice. In fact, most of the time, you won't even know he's there."

I perk up. "That's possible?"

He laughs and looks at the guys. "Anything is possible with us, Lily. Haven't you learned yet that we just make shit happen?"

It's true. They seem to be able to pull just about anything off. But this—my being with them—that's next-level stuff.

"I… I don't know what to say." I kiss him on the lips and next thing I know, Valentin and Artem are guiding me to the sofa. While I'm still standing, they unzip the back of my dress, and it slips to the floor. I wasn't wearing a bra since the dress exposed my shoulders, so all I'm left in are my tiny thong panty and high heels.

And I have to admit, in spite of all that had just happened, I feel sexy as hell. Grisha sits on the sofa in front of where I stand and reaches for my breasts by palming one and pulling the other into his mouth. His tongue on my nipple sends sparks straight through to my core, and my eyes fall closed so I can savor the sensation and let it take me away from the night's events.

One of the guys behind me—I'm not sure if it's Valentin or Artem—places his hands on my shoulders and slowly pushes my head down until my ass is in the air. Grisha sits back with my breasts in his face, carrying on with his skillful touches, no doubt contributing to the growing throb making itself known between my legs.

Now that I'm bent forward, someone's hands are smoothing over my ass, alternately taking fistfuls of my flesh, parting my cheeks, and giving me light, playful smacks.

A far cry from what they gave me my first night at the house.

Below me, Grisha opens his trousers, exposing his erection. I start to reach for it, his beautiful, hard cock with a glistening drop forming on the tip, but he slaps my hand away.

"No. Not your hand. Lower your pussy on me," he quietly demands.

I crawl up on the sofa with one leg on either side of him, and balance over his dick. His thumb flies to my clit, and I suddenly *must* have him inside me, no matter how ill-prepared I might be to handle him.

So, I part my lips with my free hand and slowly allow his tip inside. Even that much gives me pause and I hover while my pussy adjusts.

"You good, babe?" he whispers.

But before I can say anything, Valentin answers. "Art, I got her nice and juicy for you, buddy."

He's right. I lower myself, so full of Grisha's

cock I almost can't breathe. It's like the damn thing has impaled me all the way to my throat.

I hold myself there for a moment as someone's hands return to my ass, and when a tongue touches my puckered hole, I start pistoning on Grisha's dick—that's how good both things at once feel.

While I slide on his shaft, I simultaneously push my behind into the face of whoever's licking me.

Incredible.

"God, baby, your pussy's tight," Grisha groans.

Then, with a sudden movement, he lifts me clear off his cock.

"What… what the…?" I start to ask.

But he shifts me until I feel a cock pressing into my pussy from behind. A second later, I am being fucked by someone different.

Holy shit.

I realize it's Valentin, because I spot Artem out of the corner of my eye. He's pulled his own cock out of his pants and is slowly running his hand up and down the shaft.

Valentin drives into me and pulls back out, over and over, so hard that Grisha, who I'm still kneeling over, has to hold me in place. Only a minute more and I'll come so hard—

The Valentin stops.

"Hey—" I start to say.

But Grisha grabs me and pulls me back down over his cock.

Weirdest fucking game I've ever played.

I grind on Grisha, trying to get the release I desperately need. The surface of my skin buzzes in anticipation, and just as waves of pleasure start to wash over me…

Grisha pulls me off his cock. Again.

"What? What are you guys doing to me?" I cry.

Artem moves toward me until his cock presses against my lips. "There you go, baby. With my cock in your mouth, you can't complain."

He pushes inside me, nearly to the back of my throat.

I groan and try to twist my head, but I'm held in place.

Valentin leans over my back and puts his hands on my breasts. "Don't worry, darlin', we'll let you come eventually."

Fuckers.

I'm wild with need and when Valentin finally drives his cock back inside me, I clench with all my might, bouncing back on him as hard as I can. I have to come. I have to come *now*. And as I start to buck and moan, even with my mouth full of

Artem, Valentin continues to pump, giving me what I need. At last.

As I start to come down and my head droops, he pulls out *again* and turns me over to his brother. Grisha fills my pussy in one stroke, and my orgasm continues as if it were never interrupted. With hands, lips, and well, all three men enjoying my body, I'm coming over and over. And just when I can't see straight anymore, there's a pressure on my asshole and a burning sensation, and something pushes inside while Grisha's still in my pussy.

I was so not expecting *that*.

I spit Artem's dick out of my mouth. "Hey, I don't know about this—" I start to say.

But Valentin just holds himself there while Grisha reaches down to rub my clit. "Relax, baby, he whispers in my ear. You can do it."

I *cannot* do it.

But Valentin pulses so gently into my ass without going any deeper, that it actually starts to feel good. Like unbelievable. Like nothing I've ever felt before.

How is it no one ever told me about this?

"You wanna be our fuck toy, baby?" Valentin asks before pushing deeper into my ass. "We'll fill your ass, your pussy, your mouth, every day."

Well, his dirty talk is the last thing I needed. I explode into an orgasm that probably scares them all, as well as the people in the next valley over. I can't see, hear, or really even think. Only feel. Which is fine. That's what I want. Need. And crave.

It's like a cleansing. Or some kind of purification. Everything goes dark and all I can remember later is being tucked under my fluffy down comforter with a kiss on the forehead.

Oh, and someone murmured, *I love you.*

I was home. Not going anywhere.

And I'd remember to say *I love you back* in the morning.

EPILOGUE

After celebrating the new year with more sex than I knew a person could ever have, the guys said it was time to leave the Hudson Valley safe house and head back to New York City. When they saw I was a little sad to depart the place where I'd grown to love them—yes, love them—Artem promised we could come back any time we wanted. It was one of their favorite getaways.

Turns out though, they have multiple 'getaways.' Hudson Valley's just the closest.

Their others are in the Caribbean, on St. Barts. Then there's the one on the French Riviera in Cannes. Oh, they've got a home in Aspen too. Looks like I might just learn to ski.

But honestly, it was good to get back to the city. The place that had once worn me down had a shiny new luster on it, thanks to my fresh perspective. It was no longer just a fusion of long, grinding hours of work and mediocre pay from an unappreciative boss. It was no longer a place where ramen noodles were my everyday meal, where turning the heat on in my apartment was a luxury saved for the coldest nights, and where I wore the same two black dresses in rotation, hoping no one would notice.

Where the unkind words of my father followed me everywhere, like the bad memory that they were.

Or the place where I watched everyone around me have a life, where work was a thing, but not the only thing.

I've kissed my steady diet of ramen noodles goodbye, and the new apartment the guys have gotten me in the city? It has on-demand heat. I never have to be cold again.

And, yes, the guys all have keys to my apartment. In fact, most nights everyone hangs out there, like some clubhouse. It is so much fun, eating, drinking, talking, laughing, and of course getting naked. Sure, they have their own places close by, but they pretty much always want to be with me.

In an incredibly short period of time, I've stumbled into a new life. One I never dreamed I might have. I can't wait to share my good fortune with my little sisters, Charleigh and Evie. God knows those kids deserves a break.

Perhaps best of all is that the guys have backed me in opening my own events planning company. I am now in competition with my old boss, and because the guys are well-connected, I already have more clients than I can handle. And because they got me a 24/7 bodyguard, who is a real pro at sticking to the shadows, I can go about my days without wondering when the next Sergey might be waiting around a corner.

Although nothing is guaranteed. That's one of the first things the guys taught me. Despite best efforts, a person can still run into trouble. But lessening the chances of problems makes a big difference in my ability to sleep at night. Theirs too.

Is it going to be easy to be with three guys who have an... 'interesting' way of making a living? Time will tell.

My next step? To get Charleigh and Evie here with me in New York.

They have no clue about my new life, and while I'm not about to go into great detail with them over the phone, I am finally ready to tell them to get on the next plane, train, or bus and get their butts here.

"Lily! Hi!"

Charleigh always answers my calls on the first ring and it's not just because I pay for her cell phone. I'm the big sister and she knows nobody has her back like I do.

"Hey, little sis. What's all that noise in the background?"

Sounds like a toss between a marching band and a brawl.

Turns out that's pretty much what it was.

"Oh my god, Lil, Daddy's out front with someone who wants to buy a trombone. The kid is trying it out while his mother's arguing over the price. It's hilarious. Evie's over a friend's house so is missing the whole thing."

Dad's pawn shop business supported us, more or less, all our lives, but I'd do anything to get my sisters out of there and exposed to more of the opportunities the world offers.

"So Char, how's your course coming?"

I can hear her moving away from the racket in Dad's shop, and when a door softly closes, I know she's in the bathroom.

The only quiet place in the store. I'd spent a lot of time there, growing up.

It's not that I don't appreciate the hard work my dad

does to keep his business up and running. It's just that, if it were me, I wouldn't have my young daughters running around a place like that. Dad's pawn shop always tended to attract unsavory characters, many of whom are down on their luck and in need of quick cash, who are not always the kind of folks you want around your little girls.

"My course is so good, Lil, you'd be so proud. I met a new friend, Luci, who lives in Chicago. We study together and we are killing it with straight A's."

My heart swells, and my eyes tear up. Charleigh's never thought of herself as smart, and her bookkeeping course is building her confidence in a way that all my positive words never could.

"Listen, Char. When you're done with the course, I want you to come to New York with Evie. I have an extra room or could even get you your own apartment."

She gasps. "What? Lil? That's crazy."

I knew she'd have questions. And I'm ready for them.

"Look. I met a... guy." No need to tell her any more at this point. "And we're pretty serious. I'll tell you more when I see you, but I can afford to help you guys come to New York, just like I've been talking about since forever."

She's silent, taking it all in, and Valentin joins the

rest of us in the apartment with our take-out Thai dinner.

If the guys hadn't been fans of Thai food, I don't know what I would have done.

"Hey, babe," he calls.

"Who's that?" Charleigh asks in a playful voice.

I look at the other guys and put a finger to my lips. They laugh.

"Is that your new boyfriend, Lil?" she teases.

I hesitate. I hadn't spent much time thinking about exactly what to call the guys. But I guess boyfriend is good for now.

"Yeah, Char. That's Val. And we're gonna sit down for some Thai food soon. But look, think about coming to the Big Apple. You could continue with classes or go straight to work somewhere."

"Wow, Lil, that's just so—"

But she stops mid-sentence, and the shop's background noise gets louder.

Which is strange since she's in the bathroom.

What the hell's going on?

"Char, what's that noise? Is it still the kid with the trombone?"

She doesn't say anything for a few seconds, and my heart leaps into my throat. The guys, their attention directed my way, immediately sense something is wrong from my voice. Artem gestures with open hands and all I can do is look back and shrug.

Now I'm on my feet, pacing the length of the apartment. Without focusing, I look out my tall windows to Central Park, and the high rises beyond it. While I've come to love my view as a talisman of all that's possible in life, at this moment, it's not registering. I could be staring at a cinderblock wall for all the panic running through my brain.

"Char, talk to me!" I insist, trying to keep my voice under control.

There's a lot of banging, and then my sister finally speaks softly. "I don't know what's going on out there, but Daddy's shouting, and some men are yelling back at him. Someone's smashing things around the store," she whispers.

My thinking goes into overdrive while the guys circle me. "Okay, Char, stay in the bathroom and lock the door. Don't make a sound."

"Okay," she says in a voice that's starting to crack.

This is why I want to get my sisters where I can see them every day and watch over them. Because my father's never been one to look out for his kids.

"Lil, I'm scared," she whispers.

I switch the phone to speaker so the guys can hear. "I know, honey. But if you stay quiet, you'll be safe."

I look at Artem, who is frowning, and then at

Grisha and Valentin, whose faces are equally covered with concern.

"What the fuck is going on there?" Grisha asks after one particularly loud bang.

I put the phone on mute. "My dad owns a pawn shop. It sounds like a robbery or something," I tell them.

He nods. "That's what it sounds like to me too."

Oh god, oh god, oh god. I am worried for my father and his business, of course. But Dad can take care of himself. He always could.

Charleigh is a different story. She spent nearly her entire childhood hiding behind me, afraid of her own shadow. She has zero street smarts.

"Lil? It's quiet now," she says in a shaking voice.

Valentin gestures with his chin. "Tell her to open the door very slowly and to let us know what she sees."

I take the phone off mute. "Char? Look out the door. Tell me what you see."

The bathroom door clicks. Charleigh whispers. "I'm looking. From what I can see, whoever it was, is now gone. But I don't see Daddy, either." Her voice is trembling.

Shit. If my dad is in a bad way, the last thing I want is for Charleigh to find him. Thank god Evie's not there.

But there is no other way around it.

"Char, if it seems like everyone's gone, take a look

around. But keep quiet and close to the walls, okay?" I say, repeating what Artem just whispered in my ear.

Then I hear a gasp. "Oh my god, Daddy's hurt," Charleigh cries, "Lil, he's on the floor and is bleeding. What do I do? What do I do, Lil—"

And the line goes dead.

Did you like Lily's story in *My Bratva Christmas*? Ready to step into the next XXXmas holiday party?
Snow Cam Do by Layne Williams invites you to join.

Get *Snow Cam Do* here!

To learn what happens with Lily's little sister, Charleigh, check out *Cruel Promise*, A Beauty and the Bratva story, available in 2023.

Find all Mika Lane books here!

*12 Days of F*ckmas* by Kenya Wright

My Bratva Christmas by Mika Lane

Snow Cam Do by Layne Daniels

Pinched by a Grinch by Eve London

I'm USA TODAY bestselling contemporary romance author Mika Lane, and am all about bringing you sexy, sassy stories with imperfect heroines and the bad-a*s dudes they bring to their knees. And I have a special love for romance with multiple guys because why should we have to settle for just one hunky man?

Please join my Insider Group and be the first to hear about giveaways, sales, pre-orders, ARCs, and most importantly, a free sexy short story: http://mikalane.com/join-mailing-list/.

Writing has been a passion of mine since, well, forever (my first book was *The Day I Ate the Milkyway,* a true fourth-grade masterpiece). These days, steamy romance, both dark and funny, gives purpose to my days and nights as I create worlds and characters who defy the imagination.

I live in magical Northern California with my own handsome alpha dude, sometimes known as Mr. Mika Lane, and two devilish cats named Chuck and Murray. These three males also defy my imagination from time to time.

A lover of shiny things, I've been known to try new recipes on unsuspecting friends, find hiding places so I can read undisturbed, and spend my last dollar on a plane ticket somewhere.

I'll always promise you a hot, sexy romp with kick-ass but imperfect heroines, and some version of a modern-day happily ever after.

I LOVE to hear from readers when I'm not dreaming up naughty tales to share. Join my Insider Group so we can get to know each other better http://mikalane.com/join-mailing-list, or contact me here: https://mikalane.com/contact.

www.ingramcontent.com/pod-product-compliance
Lightning Source LLC
Chambersburg PA
CBHW070513200726
48293CB00007B/2520